THE BLIND HYPNOTIST

All of the characters in this book are fictitious, and any resemblance to actual persons, living or dead, is purely coincidental.

Library of Congress Cataloging in Publication Data

Lovell, Marc.
    The blind hypnotist.

I. Title.
PZ4.L89913Bl3   [PR6062.O853]   823
ISBN: 0-385-11500-8
Library of Congress Catalog Card Number 75-36600

Copyright © 1976 by Doubleday & Company, Inc.
All Rights Reserved
Printed in the United States of America
First Edition

PART ONE

PART ONE

1

Jason walked quickly. His turns were smooth when he avoided the pedestrians who strolled beside the closed shops. Dusk gathering now, lights were coming on.

The death of another summer day, Jason Galt thought. The thought surprised him. Why death instead of end?

He told himself it was because of his nervous excitement. It made him dramatise, exaggerate. And that was what the situation could do without. It had enough already.

Jason clenched his fists to counter a tingle of pleasure, and apprehension, and—yes—fear.

There was no need for that, he thought. The deal would come off. All would be slick. No detail had been overlooked.

Pleasure, yes. Fear, no. Apprehension of failure? Well, maybe. But if not success tonight, then tomorrow. But tonight was sure to be it. Third time lucky.

Jason opened his hands and with them sliced the air as he swung his arms. The damp of his palms quickly dried.

Jason Galt was tall and slim. At thirty-seven his body retained the snap of youth, like that of a dancer, or of a boxer who will never learn any more and concentrates on fighting age. He had broad, hunched shoulders. His hands were large, strong, capable; they looked to have the ability of playing a piano or picking a pocket, sculpting a cupid or killing a chicken.

Whereas most actors offstage look like waiters, Jason Galt carried with him an air of theatre. He owned a decided presence. It was in his walk, his stance when motionless, in his every gesture, and in the way he swept his gaze around, as if over the heads of vassals.

Someone had once said of Jason, "Only an amateur could look so much like a pro should." It was an apt remark.

He was approaching a corner. On it stood a police constable, hands afted, a frown ready for cars which had not yet switched on their lights.

I'll slip behind him, Jason thought. Then he decided he was being ridiculous. This continual wariness of policemen ever since he had begun planning the scheme—quite ridiculous. It could make him vulnerable.

He passed in front of the constable and said, "Good evening."

"Evening, sir," the constable said absently.

And that was equally as stupid, Jason mused sourly.

He rounded the corner and strode on, leaving the shopping district behind. The wide road was lined with tenements and warehouses, both dreary. This part of Camden Town had changed little in face and not at all in spirit since Queen Victoria was unamused by the poor.

Jason liked the area. For one thing, its griminess reminded him of the Staffordshire town in which he had grown up. For another, its sordid aspect was dramatic rather than wearying, which served him the way an observer finds the sightless satisfying and the purblind a bore, so cruel can emotion be. Thirdly, the area was always full of noise and movement, like pups in a box.

Even so, Jason would have no pangs about leaving, about moving into a home of luxury in a fashionable district. If and when the scheme came off.

When, Jason assured himself. *If* was for dreamers and Kipling.

Recalling the time he had recited that swollen verse, at a school concert, his first public appearance at the age of six, Jason smiled.

The smile worked a magic. It transformed his face. He at once looked charming, kind, innocent, looked the way disillusioned parents see the children of others, looked to have not a worry in his care.

Jason soon let the smile go. It was a muscle-shift he had little familiarity with.

Now, face in repose, Jason was the picture of solemnity, even gloom, like an illiterate watchman. Yet this detracted in no way from his handsomeness. Rather, it lent him a romantic aspect: the brooding hero.

Jason had dark eyes, a straight nose, prominent cheekbones, a square chin. The mouth was well-formed but with a slight downcast of bitterness. His brow was tall. Dark, long, shaggy hair complemented the features; it also suited Jason's windcheater, open-neck shirt and jeans. He could have passed for a student prematurely aged by dissipation.

Rounding a corner, Jason came into Shank Place. Only five of its dozen streetlamps were working, which helped hide the decay and disrepair, the sick condition of the few parked cars and the chalked obscenities.

Shank Place, a dead end, had ten houses on either side and four across the bottom. Each house stood alone—barely, a skinny metre of space between neighbours—and each had the same stucco finish, pillared portico, bay windows in three layers, front yard six feet deep.

Some houses had windows and doors blocked with corrugated iron, itself bearing rippled posters stating the property was condemned. The whole street, in fact, was condemned. But some landlords were fighting off demolition to the last compensatory penny.

Jason Galt strode across the untidy, cracked roadway, aiming for a house in the middle of the far side. Its upper and lower windows were boarded over with wood from packing cases. The centre windows had glass and curtains, and light.

Like its neighbours, the house had lived sturdily for almost a hundred years, seeming to grow stronger with time, which might have caused the wrathful human finger to press the bomb-release here instead of over the factory-object. The same thing had been happening all over Europe, however, no one having learned from the practice war in Spain.

Bomb and incendiary damage had begun the rot which time would have needed another hundred years to bring about. Neglect and the weather had done the rest.

Stucco had fallen away in great patches, like icing from a stale cake. Sills and pediments were unaligned. The door's lines of pattern were blurred by uncountable coats of paint, the latest a cheeky yellow. The two pillars leaned so far out of the true that a prolonged gaze caused alarm, like staring at a tall building against moving clouds.

Yet for Jason the house had its own peculiar charm. He would have rejected with horror a neat suburban bungalow.

And especially now, he mused, the attributes of Number Nine Shank Place were invaluable.

He clenched his fists briefly as he walked through the gateless opening in the low front wall. Going up the four steps, he unlocked the door and went inside.

"Jason?"

"Yes."

The call, female, had come from up the stairs, a broad and grand flight which rose at one side of the hallway—this a place of emptiness and bare floorboards, of echoes and the smell of damp.

The stairs were also naked. Loud thudding went up with Jason, even though he had learned to tread softly.

Jenny looked over the balustrade. She asked, "The portable?"

"Yes. They'll bring it in the morning."

Their voices contrasted oddly. Jason's was deep, resonant, caressing. Jenny's, normally high, was higher now with tension.

"I rented it for three months," Jason said.

"Why so long?"

"It's the minimum."

Nodding, Jenny turned away. She was small and pretty and shapely, a ballerina type except for her breasts, which were poutlarge. Her hair was a cap of black curls, like tarred foam. She had green eyes, a pert nose, a mouth whose oversize she contrived successfully to reduce with lipstick. The mole on one cheek looked artificial. She wore blue jeans and a sweater.

Jenny Mead had lived with Jason for two years, since she was twenty-five. They were content together. They never argued. They were not in love.

At the stairhead, Jason paused to look around. He was not yet accustomed to the change. Until three days ago, the landing had been just that, a broad area furnished only with a rug; its purpose to give access to the four doors here and to the staircase that rose to the top floor, which was long vacant and rain-sodden.

The day before yesterday, Jason and Jenny had moved the furniture from the front room out here. Now the landing was the living area: standard lamp, couch, breakfront, table and upright chairs: the things they had bought fourth-hand when moving into 9 Shank Place.

The front room was now their bedroom. Their old one at the rear was prepared as sleeping quarters for a guest. It was prepared frugally, with a simple cot and a chair, though the new drapes were extra heavy and not capable of being drawn back.

The other two doors, facing the staircase down, were of the bathroom and kitchen, a severely functional pair as unattractive as wet cats.

Jenny had gone to the couch. She was sitting tautly upright, hands clasped on her knees. She glanced at the sideboard clock.

"Yes," Jason said. "I'll be leaving soon."

"I don't like it."

"Try to relax."

Jenny gave her head a curt shake. "Can't."

"Everything's going to work out fine, Jen."

She smiled. "I'm scared." Jenny had this trick sometimes of looking solemn when happy, and the reverse.

Jason put his hands behind his back to give them a long, curing clench. He said again, "Try to relax."

"So many things could go wrong."

"No. I believe in it."

Jenny said, "I wish I had your faith."

"You do have. In me. In my talent."

"That, yes."

"Nothing can go wrong," Jason said. "How about a cup of tea?"

With their tea they sat at the table, which was set against the bannisters. Opposite stood the breakfront, beside the couch. While drinking in silence, Jason and Jenny glanced surreptitiously at the clock, each hoping the other wouldn't notice the act. Jenny's tension had transmitted itself to Jason. He was willing the clock to speed. Jenny wished the hands would freeze.

Jason forced a grin.

"Listen," he said. "Relax. Think of goodies. Think of a big colour TV instead of a measly black-and-white portable."

Jenny said, "Don't joke. It's too late for that."

He shrugged, sighing. "Anyway, it might not be tonight."

"But you think it will."

"Yes."

Jenny said a toneless, "So do I."

Jason gave a real smile, one of gratitude. "Thanks."

Openly, they both looked at the clock. Jason checked it with his wristwatch. He got up, went into the front bedroom, switched on the light and closed the door.

Jason took off and tossed aside his windcheater as he crossed to the vanity table. Lying there among jars and lotions was what looked like a handful of dark hair scooped from a barber's floor. Beside it was a tube of glue.

Jason switched on the light over the mirror. He sat on the beer-crate stool. He stared soberly at his reflection. At times, he thought, I wonder about you.

He set to work.

Five minutes later, the Vandyke beard was glued firmly into place. It was old and shabby, and therefore looked real. Not, he reminded himself, that it mattered greatly. But it would be a help if things went wrong. Which was unlikely.

He rose and stepped to a massive, furiously ugly wardrobe, swung open the doors, looked at his own half on the left.

There was little to look at. His one decent suit, a cardigan, a dufflecoat, half a dozen shirts (three to a hanger), slacks, a set of tails under a polythene bag, and a grey overcoat which had never seen better days, only newer.

The last he took out and put on. He wound a muffler once around his neck before buttoning the coat to the chin and raising its collar. From the bottom of the wardrobe he lifted a hat, a greasy dark-grey trilby with a melancholy brim. He had stolen it two weeks before in a workers' cafe.

Hat on, Jason turned to the mirror. He raised the muffler until it hid his false beard. Good, he thought.

Patting his pockets to reassure himself of the presence there of his other needs, he switched off lights and went out of the room.

Jenny was standing by the kitchen door. Head down, hands clasped, she looked like a schoolgirl waiting to go into the principal's office for chastisement.

Jason went to the head of the stairs. He moved down two steps and then halted, turning back. Something should be said, he felt. He ought to say at least a word of appreciation. This was an important moment. He ought to thank her for the times she had brought him out of depression; for the comfort and affection she had given; for the occasional financial support with her waitress job, and for having quit that job now in order to be here, to help; for putting herself in danger.

Jason found he could form none of these into words. He said, "You're a great girl, Jen."

She made no response.

Jason turned and went on down.

● ● ● ● ● ●

He got off the bus in Oxford Street. The shopping mecca was blazing light at every socket for the benefit of a handful of strollers.

It was ten o'clock. Soon the theatres would close, next the cinemas, then the pubs. By a quarter to twelve only private clubs and a few restaurants would be open. The last trains would have gone, taxies would be scarce, beat policemen would look twice at each lone walker.

Hospitals and police stations, gambling rooms and the better brothels—these never closed. Nor did that central pharmacy where registered drug addicts, ghostly in pre-shot limbo, went to fill their daily prescriptions.

As he walked down Charing Cross Road, Jason lowered the muffler. It had served its purpose, hiding the beard from any home-area acquaintance who might have seen him.

The second change Jason made in his appearance was to slump. He increased the hunch of his shoulders, set forward his head. He appeared older now; also, in the shabby hat and coat, a figure of apathy.

Traffic was light. Vehicles were outnumbered by pedestrians—mostly provincial teenagers, safe in groups, looking about them worriedly for evidence of the big city.

By Foyle's, Jason turned off into Soho. He went slowly along the narrow streets. Although still tense, he was confident. It had been a strong help, Jenny's mutual feeling that this would be the night.

Again Jason experienced a surge of gratitude, followed by annoyance at his inability to give it expression. She had been an angel, he thought. When success came (no more *if*), she would have whatever she wanted. She deserved it. Deserved the best. She had walked a long hard road to nowhere.

Jenny Mead's story was trite, a commonplace, a rule of rare exceptions. Country girl goes to metropolis in search of theatrical fame and fortune. Makes the rounds of agents and auditions. Fails after two years to get even walk-on part, place in chorus or movie crowd-scene. Tries stripping with bump and grind. Gives up in self-disgust. Too proud to face home sneers, stays on in menial work. Shares flat with other girls, rises in job from sink to table, and frequently questions sagacity of having decided against alternative of prostitution.

Yes, Jason thought, Jenny was due for a break. Perhaps she had expected one when they had met, he bragging about his stage background in order to impress the pretty girl, she politely pretending to be familiar with his name. But he was not the string she might have hoped she could pull. Her awe wore off like the finish on cheap shoes: Jason had been "resting" a long time. The affair, however, settled into a comfortable permanency.

Jason assured himself that a break Jenny would get, one way or another.

He came out of the dim streets onto Shaftesbury Avenue. It was as if he had climbed from a dungeon into sunshine. All around him were light-blaring shops and the flicker-wink bulbs of theatres.

Here the traffic was denser. Cars crawled while their occupants looked about and pointed and smiled at the brightness. Jason disliked that, for he had once done it himself and he hated to feel unoriginal. And he hated feeling small for his dislike.

After waiting for a break in the traffic, he went across the road. At a slow pace he walked until he was opposite the nearest theatre. He stopped and looked over.

Usually, the lights and sheen outside, the coziness and glamour seen through the glass doors, gave him an emotional twinge. Now he felt only an increase in his nervous excitement.

Siding the doors were large photographs. Some were of scenes from the play, some of the players. The most frequent repeat was a picture of a girl. Her name was underneath, also spelled out in bulbs on the marquee. Elsie Vanetti.

The photographs showed a strong face. It was handsome in some poses and pretty in others, depending on the lighting. It could never be plain. The features were too vital.

Elsie Vanetti had a firm jaw-line. Her mouth was broad, the lower lip full. A slight Roman curve took her nose out of the Anglo-Saxon commonplace, rallied the other features, and complemented especially the large, dark, compelling eyes, eyes under a serene brow. She had blond hair. It fell in gentle waves from a centre parting to nuzzle her shoulders and neck.

There was nothing of the painted glamour queen about Elsie Vanetti. The poses were neither wide-eyed ingenue nor open-mouthed sexpot; they were hardly poses at all. She looked calmly at the camera and seemed to be telling it, "I am an actress."

At thirty-two, Elsie Vanetti was internationally famous. Her name was familiar to people who couldn't tell you the present occupant of 10 Downing Street. She had won film festival awards in San Sebastian, Cannes, Venice, Tokyo. Her Scandinavian fan club claimed a membership of eight hundred thousand. Legitimate theatre critics loved her in London, New York and Rome. The Vanetti nose was the second most popular among seekers of plastic surgery. So famous was she that her name appeared regularly on worst-dressed-women lists in magazines which needed big-name copy for free. She might well be forgotten in a year, apart from the stage, but for the moment she glittered on a pinnacle.

Looking at the photographs, Jason smiled ruefully but without bitterness. Had any acid been there, it would have meant he was thinking about himself. His thoughts were on the girl in Shank Place.

The Vanetti story was the antithesis of Jenny Mead's, that rare exception to the dreary rule. Born in Bristol of an English mother and a Sicilian father, at eighteen she had joined a revue travelling the provincial music hall circuit. She was a chorus girl. At twenty she entered a repertory group in Manchester. For four years she worked at that weekly-play grind which has produced most of the world's great actors.

She was seen by a someone who told another someone who told ... She got a small part in a film. Terrible, the movie was deservedly killed in the West End by the poison of critical disinterest.

A Swedish director, however, liking the bit-player's quietly powerful style, plus not liking to use established stars, offered her the lead in his next film. Elsie was moving.

Two decades earlier, she would have been remade—teeth, eyebrows, hair. Certainly a new Christian name would have been created to go with the acceptable Vanetti, along with a less mundane background. But styles had changed. Sheer talent had been discovered as an asset. Elsie was allowed to use it.

After the Swedish film, in which she won the Venice award, she did a play in London, another movie, a season in Stratford, Ontario, two television specials in New York. There were more films, *Private Lives* on Broadway and in Rome, *Othello* with Olivier in the West End, three months in Manchester at ten pounds a week for old times' sake, a new Pinter at the Edinburgh Festival, and a Hollywood picture budgeted at twelve million dollars. For her part in that, she won the jinx-eyed Oscar.

Now Elsie Vanetti was back in London in a play. It was the hit of the season.

Poor Jenny, Jason thought. But still and all, good for you too, Elsie. Good for all three of us.

He looked at his watch. About ten minutes to go. These things were never precise—delay in starting, a fumble in the second act, an extra curtain.

Jason gave his attention to a narrow street which crept back into dimness from beside the theatre. Signs there said Q HERE FOR UPPER CIRCLE. Beyond, barely visible in the penumbra, a small sign above an arrow said STAGE DOOR.

A movement in the corner of his vision returned Jason's eyes quickly to the glass doors. In the deserted lobby a man had appeared. He wore a tuxedo.

Jason watched tensely, even though reason told him there was no doubt about the inevitable. When a double-decker bus lumbered interveningly by, he hurried a few steps along to regain his view.

There were three pairs of doors. The man came forward and opened one set, fixing them back via a catch at the bottom. He did the same with the other two pairs. Last, he stepped out onto the street and gazed around. Jason turned, strolled on.

In a moment he glanced behind. The man had returned inside. Jason started back.

There were people in the lobby; a handful, putting on coats, talking, staring blankly in the nothingness between one reality and another.

By the time Jason was level with the theatre, the lobby was crowded and beginning to overflow onto the street, like a honeypot with leaks.

Doors banged open at the building's side. More people came out from there. The sidewalk around the theatre became packed. A jam of taxies began to build up: large black ants clustering at the honey.

Jason waited. In a surprisingly short time, the area had thinned of theatregoers. The side street was empty. No more than half a dozen stragglers stood by the glass doors, which the man in the tuxedo was starting to close.

The marquee lights went out.

Jason crossed the road. He walked to a place directly opposite the alley which led to the stage door. There was a doorway, comfortingly dark. He stepped into it with a pleasant feeling of familiarity.

Jason had waited here five times, just as on five previous occasions he had watched that exodus and closing at the front. He knew exactly how many people would leave by the alley.

First would come five performers, three of them female. Second were the two stage hands. Third, the electrician. Fourth, the two dressers, little fat women who looked like chars. Fifth, the man in the tuxedo. Sixth, Miss Elsie Vanetti. Seventh and last, together, the stage-door keeper and the stage manager. Jason knew every face.

The star had usually been by herself. In this Jason found nothing odd. Whereas the average person would expect a celebrated actress to always have an entourage of admirers, hangers-on, agents and pressmen, Jason knew that it was lonely on the pinnacle.

On two of the five occasions, last night and the night before that, Jason had gone down the alley after the fifth departure. He had been ready to act. But Elsie Vanetti had not, after all, been alone.

The first time, one of the dressers had come hurrying back, flustered, to give the star a message. Last night, Elsie Vanetti had been accompanied by a female friend who apparently had gone backstage after the show.

You just never knew, Jason mused. That human element had to be allowed for. This might be the night, for instance, when a constable takes a notion to come around checking doors.

Jason twitched. He decided on a slight change of plan—or rather, position.

He went swiftly across the street and into the alley mouth. It was smooth brickwork all the way, with flagstones beneath. It smelled of urine, despite, or to spite, a sign at the beginning saying COMMIT NO NUISANCE.

The end of the alley opened up into a yard. It was the size of a large room. There were garbage cans, crates, tall fragments of scenery. Light came from one naked bulb. This was above a door in a corner, a door up a short flight of steps, themselves balustraded with a writhe of tubular steel.

Still moving quickly, Jason went to a wall-leant stack of scenery sections. There was ample space behind. It was where he had waited on the two previous nights. From this position, he had a clear view of the stage door.

In another minute, it opened.

The performers came out single file. Each threw back a cheery good night, which was answered by a hoarse voice. The doorkeeper.

In swift succession appeared the stage hands, the electrician and the two dressers. After a pause came the tuxedo man, now bundled up as if for an arctic winter.

Next would be the star.

Jason took a deep breath, wiped his damp palms on his coat, readied himself. His perceptions were divided between the door and the street noises.

From beyond the door he heard a woman's voice. He recognised it, knowing it mainly from the performance of the play he had attended—as much to familiarise himself with the other players as to study the star.

The door opened.

Elsie Vanetti appeared.

She was medium height and firmly made; another five pounds and she would have been on the verge of plumpness. She wore a fawn-coloured, belted raincoat, one pocket of which bulged with a purse. Her shoes were plain moccasins. She wore dark glasses. Tied under her chin was a green headscarf; hair billowed from below it like yellow wool.

Except for the sunglasses, Elsie Vanetti might have been a secretary or a suburban housewife.

She said, "Good night, Bill."

The hoarse voice answered respectfully, "Good night, Miss Vanetti."

The door closed.

Jason moved out of his hiding place. He had five minutes, he reckoned, ten at most. But he could not hurry, must not hurry. Whatever happened he had to take his time.

Elsie Vanetti had paused halfway down the steps. She was gazing around, as if with expectation. Jason saw her shoulders move high, then sink.

He went forward.

The actress saw him. She stared; stiffened; semi-relaxed.

Jason went on to the foot of the steps. He was in his old-man crouch. He made a polite, token lift of his hat and asked, voice low:

"Are you one of the girls in the show, young lady?"

Shrewd, this, an idea of which Jason was proud. The pinnacle holder is responsible for much of his own loneliness. If he didn't maintain a hands-off attitude, he would spend a good deal of his time being pestered by over-eager fans, brash collectors of celebrities and those who think a public name is a public property.

Evidently assured by the lack of recognition, Elsie Vanetti nodded.

Jason said, "I thought so."

"What is it?" Her voice was melodious, attractive.

"The thing is," Jason said, "I found a piece of jewellery."

"Oh?"

He put a hand in his pocket and brought out the bauble. He was calmer now. The waiting was over. He was doing what he knew so well.

"I found it in the alley. It might be yours."

Elsie Vanetti said, "I don't think so. I haven't missed anything."

"Look," Jason said. He held up the trinket. It was a Woolworth-value stone in a wire claw and suspended from two inches of chain.

The actress came on down to the foot of the steps. She was a yard from where Jason stood. He moved closer. The bauble he dangled from its chain and held level with the girl's eyes.

"Pretty," she said.

"Yes. Not worth anything, of course. But it might have sentimental value."

This was a further allayer of suspicion. It said, in effect, I am not after money.

Due to the slight movement of Jason's hand, the bauble was moving gently, rhythmically. Its polished surface caught the light from the naked bulb and gave off tiny jets of reflection. These flicked across the lenses of Elsie Vanetti's glasses.

She said, "It's nice."

"Yes. See how it catches the light."

Jason had changed the timbre of his voice. It had become deeper yet gentler. It caressed. He used it at a deliberate speed.

"It's fascinating, isn't it? It's soothing. It creates an optical illusion. Concentrate on it and you will see what I mean."

Elsie Vanetti nodded slowly. "Yes."

"The lights seem to form a continual line. Concentrate."

"Yes."

"Don't you agree," Jason said gently, "that is very much like the feeling of approaching sleep? Sleep. When you are feeling sleepy. Very tired. When you are longing for sleep."

"Well, yes," the actress said softly.

Jason sighed. He was winning. The subject's attention was held and her motor output restricted. It was going to be as easy as he had known, remembering the young chorus girl of twelve years ago.

He said, "Sleep. It is like sleep. When you are aching for sleep. So very very tired. So sleepy, so drowsy, that you can hardly keep your eyes open. Do you agree?"

Elsie Vanetti's head gave an almost imperceptible nod. Beyond the tinted lenses of her glasses, her eyelids looked heavy, swollen.

"Longing for sleep," Jason crooned. "Sleep, lovely sleep. It would be so wonderful if only you could close your eyes, find peace in sleep."

With more firmness in his voice, he asked, "Is that right?"

Her lips moved.

Jason said, "Speak up, please."

She whispered, "Yes."

"Yes. And I, your friend, am going to let you sleep."

From the other side of the stage door sounded a slam and a hoarse laugh.

Jason tensed. His legs and stomach muscles stiffened to a rigidity like trembling wood. He was alarmed at the accompanying thought-command: Run.

The desire of his spirit was stronger. Ignoring the panic of logic, he went on speaking to Elsie Vanetti in a low, assuring voice. He resisted the urge to hurry. Haste would be as destructive as an interruption.

And an interruption seemed imminent. Another voice had joined that of a hoarse laugh. Jason knew the matching persons—doorkeeper and stage manager. He pictured them standing together while shuffling into their coats.

Did he have one minute left? Two? Three?

"Elsie," he said, using her given name for the first time, "I am going to let you close your eyes. Would you like that?"

Her whispered affirmative was as faint as a sigh.

"Very well," Jason said. "Close your eyes."

His tension increased. This was the moment. The preparation had not been as long as he would have liked. Lips apart, Jason stared through the lenses at the girl's eyelids.

Slowly, they lowered.

Elsie Vanetti was in a light hypnotic trance.

Jason shuddered. His tension eased back down to the medium level. This equalled the stage of his present progress. Capture completed, the rest was escape.

Laughter sounded from beyond the door.

Jason slipped the bauble in his pocket as he moved to the girl's side. "I am taking your arm," he said, matching action to words.

There was no expression on Elsie Vanetti's face. She might have closed her eyes for a spell of inconsequential thought.

Putting forward pressure on her arm, Jason said, "Let us walk." His tone, only lightly tinged with authority, suggested that a stroll was most desirable. Her trance was too delicate for commands.

They moved off. Side by side they crossed the yard and entered the alley. Elsie Vanetti walked slowly and carefully, her steps measured.

From behind came a click.

Jason swung his head nervously. The door had been opened; but was merely ajar, a two-inch strip of light showing.

Turning back, Jason said, "How pleasant to walk. It is exactly what you wanted to do. It makes you happy, just walking."

His nervousness had lingered. Its fingers tapped at him now as the alley ended. He was torn between wanting to get away from the danger behind, and to pause here in order to check the street for safety. He chose the former.

They stepped out of the alley—and directly into the path of a hurrying man.

Gasping, Jason pulled Elsie to a stop.

At the penultimate moment of collision, the man made a neat side-swerve. He went on, glancing back at the couple with a frown.

Looking but not seeing, Jason insisted to himself. There would be no memory of facial details, perhaps no memory of that mini-event, the man's mind enclosed by the urgency of his errand.

Jason scanned the street. It was quiet. He turned Elsie away from the blare of Shaftesbury Avenue. They began again to walk, heading into the gloom of Soho.

Jason talked. He told the actress repeatedly how much she was enjoying the stroll. Speech was vital. There was always the risk of a lightly entranced subject slipping into real sleep. It could happen to the actress, even walking. She would fall.

Jason kept up his stream of talk until, two streets from the theatre, they reached the shop he had decided on previously. It had a deep, dark entranceway. He led Elsie in and to the back.

Jason's tension began to drain away. The rest of the escape was mechanics. He would take off the girl's glasses and scarf, and put on her head—tucking in the hair—the cloche hat he carried in his pocket. He would remove his beard. They would walk on, just another couple on their way home from the theatre. Outside a large Goodge Street pub, which by that time would be ushering out its customers, they would get a taxi and go to within half a mile of Shank Place, Jason the while talking in a rambling, semi-drunken way for the driver's benefit and to keep the actress awake. Last, a walk, and home.

Jason smiled. He was confident now. He knew he had won.

2

The bedroom was small and neat and girly, like a kitten. One wall hoarded pop-star posters. There were dolls and the latest in near-pornographic fiction on shelves. Sliding doors back, the closet showed extra-mod garments as packed as a sliced loaf.

The room's owner lay asleep under a sheet, showing only her face of cute features and slurred cosmetics. Her open mouth was formed in a smile of satisfaction. She looked to be in her late teens or early twenties.

Beside her, naked on top of the covers, sprawled Hull Rainer. One hand cuddled the nape of his neck, the other held a cigarette. His smile was as smug as the girl's.

A good-looking man, Hull Rainer, attractive in that pretty-boy way that had gone out of vogue in the acting profession. Which, typically, Hull refused to believe. He blamed his resting periods on everything from his agent's uselessness to vague convictions that he was being plotted against for this reason or that.

When Hull did work, it was in motion pictures and television. If his name was known to the general public, it was mainly in connexion with his wife. He was sometimes referred to, inevitably, and cruelly, as Mr Vanetti.

Hull had a smooth round face with a snub nose, curvaceous lips of blatant sensuality, eyes as large and appealing as sunset. His wavy black hair was unfashionably short; a front lock fell forward onto his brow with a contrived casualness.

He had a small frame, yet strong and amply padded with muscle. The bodybuilder's art showed in lats and triceps and abdominals. A sunlamp tan glowed attractively everywhere save the loins, the whiteness of which set off the tan. Sauna pores plus manicure and pedicure told the rest. It was a pampered body.

Hull Rainer, born Albert Green thirty-two years ago, drew on his cigarette lazily. He thought that, all things considered, it was not a bad life. And sooner or later jobs would be more plentiful.

He glanced aside at the girl. Her name was Ann or Nan, he wasn't sure which. They had met for the first time three hours before. Hull had picked her up with ease in a wine bar after, "Excuse me, aren't you April Shire who poses for the Grant Model Agency?" The approach had worked for him more times than he could remember. It had the efficacious flattery missing from the haven't-we-met-before ploy.

Pizza and a bottle of wine had followed. Ann/Nan was sold the rest of the way past flattery by being with a real live actor, one whose face she was persuaded to believe she had seen often on big and little screens. Bed was assured, as was an eager-to-please performance.

Hull noted the girl's smile of satisfaction. He nodded with phony complacency and sent a long stream of cigarette smoke toward the ceiling.

A good lover is a man to whom the climax is of secondary interest. The reverse is true of the bad lover. Both are selfish. One goes charging in pursuit of his intense, brief pleasure without a thought for his partner; the other is subconsciously concerned with the future, wanting double pleasure—the act of love now, the partner's adoration and gratitude later. In his case of good-lover Hull Rainer, however, the procedure was well to the mental fore, not subconscious.

Reaching to the ashtray on the bedside table, Hull noticed a clock there. It gave the time as almost twelve. He wondered if he should be making tracks for home, or wake Ann/Nan for another bout.

Then, stubbing out his cigarette, Hull remembered. He groaned faintly and slapped his brow.

The anniversary.

Today was the seventh anniversary of his marriage to Elsie. He had promised he would be at the stage door to meet her, to take her home for a cozy little supper.

How could he have been so bloody stupid? he semi-fumed. As if things weren't bad enough on the domestic scene. Not dangerously bad, of course, but prickly.

Hull got quietly off the bed. He knew there was no hope of reaching home before midnight, so that at least the anniversary day still lived, but the sooner he returned the better.

While dressing, topping off with a slick modern suit and a cravat, Hull worked on thinking up a reasonable excuse. A car accident?

Caught in a two-hour traffic jam? Witnessed a brawl and had to make a statement at the police station? Got taken for a ride by little green men in a flying saucer?

Hull smiled. He was not overly perturbed.

Anyway, he thought, the excuse had to be one which didn't need proof. You never knew with Elsie. She might just take it into her head to check.

Putting on his shoes, Hull decided.

An old lady. Badly dressed. She fainted on the pavement. Got her a cab and took her home. Wretched little place in the East End. Couldn't find it again if you paid me. Settled her in and made a cup of tea.

Yes, he thought. Elsie would go for that one. The poignant bit. "Hearts and Flowers" on a violin. She would even give him an A for kind effort.

Hull went into the living room. He looked around for writing materials. As earlier, he was struck by the luxuriousness of the small flat, particularly as it belonged to a girl of Ann/Nan's age. Daddy, she had said, was in Lloyd's.

She was someone who should be cultivated, he told himself.

He found pad and pen, wrote a note saying he would be in touch, jotted down her telephone number and put that slip of paper inside his left sock, a trick he had used successfully for years. Not that he knew for certain that Elsie ever searched his pockets; but it was best to be safe.

He let himself out and went downstairs. His open MGB stood at the kerb, seat tilted forward against dew. He got in and drove off with a masculine flourish.

Hull's cheer abated as he sped through the quiet streets of Hampstead. He felt abused at having to hustle home like a servant. Sullenly, slowing the car, he mused: Who the hell does she think she is anyway? She's just had the breaks, that's all.

Albert Green became Hull Rainer the day he was accepted for RADA—the Royal Academy of Dramatic Art. He was a glib student with an undoubted acting gift. He was popular, worked hard, and left school sharing his peers' and teachers' opinion that he would go far.

That first year he appeared in a TV series and got two non-speaking roles in motion pictures. He was offered a part in a stage play but turned it down—the money wasn't good enough. Other TV and film work followed. He never fluffed lines and he agreed with everything the director said. His parts gradually grew larger.

When he and Elsie met, in a television studio, they were on career par. When they married, two years later, Elsie was midway to her pinnacle. Hull had begun to mark time.

He had come into the professional world at the end of an era that wanted his pretty-boy clean-cut image. Now that was out. The parts he did land were by way of being a slight send-up of the type he projected. He was stereotyped.

Domestically, all was serene. The Rainers got along well together, liked the same things, were of similar political bent, shared the view that the population explosion should be taken seriously. Hull, moreover, put an end to Elsie's wastage of earnings. He was good with money. Curbing her frivolous purchasing, he made wise investments, opened a joint checking account and hired an expert to make out tax returns.

All seemed well. It was three years before Hull began to seek the beds of others. Elsie was climbing, climbing.

The MGB moved along Bayswater Road. Hull flipped away a cigarette and swung the wheel, turning off at Lancaster Gate. He turned again and ramped down to the garage under an apartment building. Minutes later, he was entering the flat.

It was spacious and comfortable. Every colour and piece and fitment was no less modern than a fresh newspaper. The chrome was as rich as the ebony, the convenience as thorough as the cleanliness, the silence as deep as the carpeting. Modernity even stretched to window dressing, the blind leading the drape.

Four steel-and-leather couches in a square formed the center of the large living room. Op art stared without spirit but with promise of financial return from three walls. The other wall, mostly glass, looked out over Hyde Park, a bucolic scene which might have been a hundred miles from the city.

The flat had been in darkness, which Hull thought odd. If Elsie went to bed when he was out, she always left the lights on. He prowled. Softly he went into the master bedroom. The bed, king-size, was unchanged from the neatness left by the maid.

Hull shrugged. Obviously, he thought, Elsie had gone from the theatre to a restaurant or one of the clubs where colleagues gathered.

This was good, he mused, heading for the kitchen. He could actually come out on top. Their positions would be switched. *He* would be the injured party.

Preparing hot chocolate, smiling, Hull decided he would say he'd arrived at the stage door five minutes late—after probing to find out her actions. He had come straight home, expecting her to be here. He had waited and waited. He felt pretty hurt about it, as a matter of fact. In case she had forgotten, this was their wedding anniversary.

Yes, that would work beautifully. No nastiness, of course. Just a bit of sulk and eye-wincing. Great.

Hull finished his chocolate and went into the living room. He circled the walls, humming. By a mirror he stopped. The hum faded as he gazed at his reflection. His eyes became anxious. He changed position, moving closer and back, standing sideways, raising and lowering his chin; at all times watching his face.

No, he thought with firmness but not sure of verity. No, there was no sign of age. He could easily pass for twenty-five. Even younger.

Abruptly turning away, he went to a couch. He sat. He forgot his reflection, his doubt. Amused, he began experimenting with various poses of dejection.

The next he knew, he was sitting up creakingly from an uncomfortable sprawl.

He had fallen asleep. Feeling chilled and rotten, he looked at his watch. It was past three in the morning. He sat on for a moment, dozily listening to a hum of silence.

He went through to the bedroom. It was still deserted. No thought did he give to this until he had changed into pyjamas and robe.

With a cigarette he went to stand at the living-room window. The most likely answer, he told himself, was that Elsie had gone to stay with a friend for the night. She was putting him in the kennel. He was not surprised. There had been something about her this past week or two, as if she was building up to something.

Hull realised now that he'd had a feeling about tonight, vibes that it was going to be a climax of sorts. He wondered if that was why, without being aware of it, he had picked up Ann/Nan—to avoid going to the theatre. Certainly he had not gone out with the intention of picking up a girl.

Seeing a car race by below on Bayswater Road, seen but not heard through the double-glazing, Hull found another answer to Elsie's absence. She could have got knocked down while getting a taxi. The taxi itself could have been in an accident. There were, in fact, many answers, all unconnected with himself.

Hull yawned. He turned from the window and stubbed out his cigarette, musing:

Bed now, worry later. In daylight, telephone friends. If no dice, call hospitals. It would all come out right.

As he went into the bedroom, Hull was thinking about the smooth body of the insurance broker's daughter.

3

Jason Galt became seriously interested in hypnotism when a first-year medical student. Previously, he had been intrigued by the subject as a distant, poor and slightly disreputable relation of medicine. And, like the average layman, he saw it in terms of the mystical.

Of the last notion he was quickly disabused. The hypnoidal trance was firmly rooted in the truth of physiology and psychology. Magic had no part in it. As real and natural as a headache caused by anxiety, it had been used by Freud and was still being used by eminent men of science.

Yet it was understandable, the putative supernatural element. For thousands of years witch-doctors and their like had employed hypnotism—without, however, knowing the real source of their power. They, and others, thought it magical. Combining body gyrations to fix the attention, with monotonous chanting and drumbeats, the shaman was able to reduce his victim to pliable somnambulism. It explains the occult-seeming success of the witch-doctor's curse. He tells the victim he is going to die. Accepting this totally under hypnosis, the victim turns his face to the wall. Just as there is faith-healing, so is there faith-dying.

The showmanship of Mesmer was no help, nor such names as Svengali and Rasputin, nor the hypnotist's insistence on the glaring eye and the elaborate hand-motion. It was only when scientists started to ease out the charlatans that hypnosis began to be viewed, hesitantly, as a natural phenomenon of mind and body. But it had yet to achieve total respectability and acceptance.

In his very first attempt at inducing a trance, Jason was successful. He was an ardent convert from that moment on.

It was at about this time that he found another interest, one only fractionally less in strength. Theatricals. The stage fascinated him as if it were his own bauble, that twinkling promise of peace and satisfaction. He joined the university's drama group and an extra-mural play-reading society.

What time Jason did not spend in practicing and researching hypnotism, he spent playing at being an actor. So much so, that at the end of his second school year he was told by his anatomy professor that he was wasting his time in general medicine. Jason left.

He studied for a year with a hypnotist in London, then for eighteen months with a hypnotherapist in Vienna. He was building up valuable experience, though he had no positive idea of where it would take him, or even where he wanted to go.

This was resolved on his return to England. An American hypnotist, whose act relied heavily on humour, was playing to full houses at the Palladium. Jason saw how to bring together his two loves in a marriage which would not only be sound but also profitable.

He worked out a stage routine, went to see an agent, finally got booked into a small night-club for a weekend. His act didn't meet with the triumph he had envisioned. Neither, however, was it a flop. He got other club dates, a night here, a week there.

His agent and fellow artistes advised him that his routine lacked something. He should either use much more showmanship, or go in for more comedy. Jason resisted. Showmanship meant flowing robes, a beard, manic gestures, all the trappings of mysticism which he loathed in connexion with his calling. Comedy was the reverse slander.

But after two years of stagnation in the North, and seeing how well other stage hypnotists were doing, Jason changed his mind. As the lesser of two evils, he settled on humour.

At once his gigs improved. The rise continued until he won top billing with a revue touring the provincial music halls. He was in real theatres at last.

Twice nightly, immaculate in white tie and tails, Jason would stride onto that haven called the proscenium arch. The house lights on, he would tell the audience he wanted co-operation in an experiment.

"When I give the signal," he said, "I'd like you all to close your eyes and clasp your hands on top of your heads, fingers intertwined. Like this. Next, again on cue, I want you to turn the hands, palms upward. So."

Jason gave the signal. Perhaps half the audience participated correctly, not without self-consciousness and giggles, and perhaps one third of these were genuinely concentrating.

Jason said, "Make your minds blank. Think of nothing. Just listen carefully to what I say."

He told the participators that their hands were locking together; locking tighter; that they were locked; that no matter how hard the people tried to break the grip, they would fail, until given another signal.

"Now," he said. "Open your eyes and try to separate your hands."

There followed a continuous two- or three-minute laugh as the more suggestible of the genuine participators, their faces absurd in surprise, cavorted in the attempt to free themselves.

After giving the signal for release, Jason invited his subjects up onto the stage. Twenty or so accepted. Again using mass hypnosis, he put them into a light trance and asked them to recite a nursery rhyme. The failures or fumblers he sent back to their seats. The others he proceeded to put through various antics, though for the more complex acts he concentrated on his stooge.

Nearly all public displays of hypnotism use an audience plant. This makes one-quarter true the charge that such demonstrations are phony. But the stooge is not pretending when he kicks wildly at the dog supposedly snapping at his ankles, or tries to climb the curtain to escape a lion, or puts on an invisible coat, or cries at sad news he thinks he has been given. He is truly entranced. His use is simply a time-saving convenience. The operator could do as well with real members of the audience, but induction would take longer and be boring as entertainment. The stooge, having often been hypnotised by the operator, has with him the necessary rapport for fast entrancement.

Jason's act was popular, and, flatteringly, not only with the seat-buying public. There was always a backstage audience in the wings. Often an electrician or prop-man, succumbing to suggestion, would start slapping non-existent ants off his legs, and one of the girls travelling with the show, in the chorus, had to avoid the wings because of her extreme suggestibility.

All was fine with the world of Jason Galt. He had his calling and the stage. He had sufficient money. He had romance for the asking among show girls or stage-door Joanies, and he asked. That he was doing nothing to further the cause of hypnotism troubled him on occasion, but, he told himself, a price had to be paid somewhere.

All was fine until a tabloid blared about dangerous after-effects. Some people who had been hypnotised onstage, the paper stated, had not been properly brought out of their trances. They were acting strangely, were suffering, were causing concern.

Suddenly every part of the country had people claiming to be in post-hypnoidal trouble. Questions were asked in the House of Commons. A lobby began for the banning of all public performances of hypnotism.

Not waiting for what seemed the inevitable, Jason's producer cancelled his act and replaced him with a TV comic. Jason was on the streets.

For a year he tried to get back into the theatre—in any capacity. He lived on his savings and then the dole. Wearying at last of rejection, he accepted a humble position as assistant to a psychoanalyst.

The doctor, whose degree was academic, not medical, had a strong interest in the use of hypnotism in analysis, which was becoming common, yet had no knowledge of the art himself. Jason's task was to supply that lack.

The association, though amicable, was not a total success in the consulting room. With two people to contend with, transference was difficult for the patient, who, additionally, had to adjust in midtrance from one controlling voice to another. But Jason and the doctor persisted.

One day, Jason met a patient by chance in a bar. The man's neurosis had been bared as to causation, yet the symptoms continued. Getting an idea, Jason took the man home, put him into a deep trance and then told him to forget the childhood incident which created his anxiety, ordered him to erase it from his mind.

Later, Jason told his employer what he had done. The doctor was furious. It was covering up again, he said, what had taken so long to uncover. They had an argument. Jason quit.

(Years afterwards they met, made up and had a drink. The doctor said, "You know, that patient, he never did come back.")

Soon, borrowing money, Jason rented an office and set himself up as a lay consultant in minor psychiatric problems. Ninety per cent of his work dealt in helping people, through hypnosis, to give up cigarettes. That, as a non-medical practitioner, he was able to advertise, helped bring him business. The same fact, unfortunately, helped the dozens of other hypnotherapists, most of whom had dubious qualifications but a glamorous facade.

This lasted for three years. Jason was getting nowhere. He gave up the consultancy and began an extended period of worklessness interspersed with part-time jobs. His constant thought was: What next?

Nothing. Not until some time after he had moved with Jenny into the house in Shank Place.

● ● ● ● ● ●

"There isn't a mention."

Jason nodded. "I told you."

"Funny. You'd think it would be."

"It might not even be till tonight, late, when she doesn't show up at the theatre."

"Could be, yes. If her husband's away or something."

Jenny and Jason had been saying similar things to each other for the past half hour, ever since Jason had come in from his quick trip out to buy the morning newspapers. Neither he nor she was aware of the repetition.

They were in their living room, the ex-landing. Jenny sat at the table. It bore a jumble of breakfast dishes and defeated newspapers. Wearing a faint smile of nervousness, Jenny was reading again the page she had already scoured twice.

Jason, on the couch, was telling himself he should have been prepared for a lack of development. The radio newscasts, to which they had been listening since 7 A.M., had not included a reference to Elsie Vanetti.

Jenny asked, "Would they keep it a secret?"

"No. For what reason?"

She made a don't-know gesture, flipping a hand sideways. Her face was pale. There were wedges of duskiness under her eyes like week-old bruises. She went on reading, searching.

The landing was silent apart from the radio's mumble, the rustle of newsprint and the scraping sound created by Jason.

He was at work. On his knees he held a brick, an ordinary house brick which he had picked up at a building site. On it he rubbed the soles of a pair of flat-heeled women's shoes, slowly, giving a minute to each. The chore was absorbing. He was glad.

"No," Jenny said. "Not a word."

"I told you."

"Very odd."

"Not really."

Jenny sat back and folded her arms, nestling them under her breasts like skinny twins. She looked small and in need of protection. The impression increased as she continued to sit watching Jason.

In a moment Jenny said, "Poor girl."

Jason looked up quickly. "What d'you mean?"

Jenny gave a slight start, as if at an unexpected flash of light. On her lower face a blush rapidly came, rapidly went. She said, a mumble:

"I was just thinking."

"About what?"

Jenny straightened, lost her expression of apology, smiled. "That poor girl. I'm sorry for her."

"She's all right," Jason said. He looked down again but didn't go on with his work. "Don't worry about Elsie."

"I do."

"She won't come to any harm."

"I know. Not real harm. It's not that."

"What, then?"

"I'm worried about the whole thing."

Jason sighed. He leaned down to push brick and shoes under the couch. Sagging back, drooping, he said:

"It's going to be fine, Jen. The worst part was last night. It came off, as you know."

"Yes, but I don't mean that either," Jenny said. As if with effort, she plucked one arm away from her body. Off the table she lifted a crust of bread. She tapped her chin with it and scraped it on her bottom teeth. Jason had cured her of smoking, but not of the need of small comforts.

"All right, Jen," Jason said, his voice coming from a far, cool place. "Tell me what you mean."

Jenny smiled. "I think it's immoral."

That made a silence. The silence increased the discomfort Jason felt for the statement. It should have been talked into submission at once.

He and Jenny had discussed every aspect of the affair except this. He had not even discussed it with himself. It was a niggle that Jason had kept under control, sometimes with brutality. He needed to be strong. It was so easy to get mawkish, then weak, then defeatist.

Jenny spoke first. She said, "You must agree on that, dear."

Jason rose swiftly, irritably. He went to stand with his rump pressed on the bannister rail. Feeling better now that he was looking down at Jenny, and, for some reason, that he was looking at her with turned head, he said airily, "A little, yes."

"It is immoral," she pushed.

"In a way."

"Oh, come on."

"Okay okay," Jason said, discomfort fading like a panic in error. "It's immoral."

"Thanks."

"I know it. We both know it. It's understood. Why bring it up now?"

Jenny bit a piece of the crust of bread. Chewing, she said, "I want you to know how I feel."

"It's a bit too late to start getting doubts, sweet." He always used endearments when he was unsympathetic. "Unless you want me to call the whole thing off."

"I'm worried, that's all. What we're doing is wrong."

"Criminal, yes."

"We have no right to do this to that poor girl."

Jason looked at the sideboard clock. "Darling, I do wish you wouldn't keep saying 'poor girl.'"

"I'm sorry for her."

"I'm sorrier for you and me."

"We're not exactly living in the depths of misery, dear."

Jason gave a snort-grunt.

Pointing her crust, Jenny asked, "Would you really call the whole thing off? If I asked, would you?"

"No," Jason said shortly. He was still looking at the clock. He asked, for the third time that morning, "When does the news come on TV?"

Jenny answered as she had before: "Ten."

"I can't wait. I'd better get started. If it's mentioned, tell me about it later. Don't disturb me."

"I know."

"Don't let anyone in the house."

"No," she said patiently.

Jason eased himself off the bannister rail. He ran his hands first over his long hair, next down his sweater, last along the hips of his jeans. With a smile to Jenny, he went to the door of the second bedroom and entered softly.

● ● ● ● ● ●

Elsie Vanetti lay on top of the bed. She was fully dressed, apart from her shoes. Legs drawn up and arms crossed, she lay sleeping on her side like a child. Her mouth was open. The pillow was streaked with strands of her hair.

Jason went to the bed and bent over. He began to talk to the actress quietly, bringing her from real sleep to light-trance somnambulism. He told her to sit up. She obeyed, moving slowly. Her eyes were still closed.

Jason took her hand, drew her off the bed and led her over to a chair. He had her sit. On her feet he put a pair of slippers belonging to Jenny.

Elsie sat in a forlorn slump, head down, hands untidily in her lap. Her raincoat was twisted and creased. Her hair fell in tangles like lengths of cheap string.

"Elsie," Jason said in his most caressing tone, "you have had a good sleep and are refreshed. You feel fine. You feel cheerful. You are relaxed and at your ease."

The girl's face produced a modicum of expression, of vitality, while her body lost some of its laxness. Tentatively, her hands met in a loose clasp.

Jason asked, "Are you hungry?"

"No"—a whisper.

"Please remember what I told you before. If you're hungry or thirsty, or if you want to go to the bathroom—say so. If you are alone, find the door and knock. Understand?"

"Yes."

"Do you think you could find the door?"

"Yes."

"Good girl," Jason said. He stood for a moment, looking at his subject with satisfaction, before starting again to talk. He set about putting Elsie into a medium trance.

After two minutes he said, "Behind you, in a vase, are three flowers. A rose, a tulip, a carnation. What are they?"

When Elsie had repeated the names, Jason went on, "In a while, you will find it very difficult to remember what flowers are in the vase. Be assured of that. You will find it difficult."

After more monotonous speech, Jason asked Elsie to name the

flowers. Her lips moved without a sound, her closed eyes creased with effort.

"Never mind," Jason said, pleased. Elsie was in a medium trance. She looked no different from before.

Merely to strengthen his power over the subject, Jason told her that when she heard him snap his fingers she would be able to recall the flowers by name. He snapped his fingers.

Elsie said, "A rose, a tulip, a carnation."

Jason moved on to the next step.

In ten minutes the actress was in a deep trance. To make sure of this, Jason took a pin from the waistband of his jeans and told his subject that her right hand had been treated with a local anesthetic, that she could feel no pain there.

Taking the hand, he separated the index finger and jabbed it deeply with the pin. There was no reaction. He could have been spiking a sausage.

"Open your eyes," he said, turning away and sitting on the bed. As he put the pin away, he thought he would probably not need it again. In future, induction to the profound state would be faster and simpler. Already an emotional relationship was developing between operator and subject.

What this relationship was exactly, Jason didn't know. Nor did anyone else. It constituted one of the remaining mysteries in hypnotism, and the greatest. There were many theories, two of which towered above the others.

One said the subject believed his controlling voice to belong to a parent; that, in point, he had regressed to childhood. The theory explained the amazing malleability of the hypnotised. Go into a sleeplike trance, yes, but why obey all orders, ridiculous and otherwise? Because obeying is part of security.

The second theory said the subject believed he was listening to the voice of his own mind. If so, then naturally he obeyed his own commands.

Jason lay back on the bed and put both hands behind his neck. In this particular case, he was hoping for and working on the first theory. While researching Elsie Vanetti, he had learned that she and her late father had been unusually close.

Jason smiled at the ceiling. He was not dismayed at the amount of work ahead—twelve or fourteen hours today, same tomorrow, and the next day, and the next . . .

Slow, painstaking work. No detail to be overlooked. The details known about, that is. All was impossible. But 90 per cent successful would do the trick.

Turning his head, Jason looked at Elsie. Her eyes were open. She was watching him. Eyes always go to the animate—a fly if nothing else is available. The living have need of the living.

Elsie's eyes were dull. She might have been looking at a piece of wood.

Jason asked, "What is the last thing you remember, Elsie?"

In a lingering voice the actress said, "A man."

"Yes? Go on."

She became less tired-seeming. Her manner was different now from that of the light trance. The deeper, the more like true wakefulness.

"An old man," she said. "In the yard. He had some jewellery. A shiny thing. Someone had lost it."

"Can you picture that man?"

"Oh, yes."

"Right," Jason said. "Now you will eradicate that picture from your mind. You will forget the man entirely. The look of him and the fact of him—forget."

"Very well."

After a pause, Jason asked, "What is the last thing you remember?"

The actress blinked. Jason wasn't sure, but he thought a tremor worked its way over her body, like a fought shiver.

She said, "Something evil."

Jason tensed, staring. Slowly he pushed himself up to a sitting position. He ordered, "Repeat that."

"Something evil," Elsie murmured.

"Where?"

"Everywhere. All around. Inside and out. Something evil."

Abruptly Jason relaxed. He realised that Elsie must be referring to the play in which she was acting. In it, she portrayed a rich girl whom her guardian and his family were trying to drive insane.

"We will come to that in a minute, Elsie. You have forgotten one or two things."

"Sorry."

"But first of all, let me ask you this: do you recall an old man with a piece of jewellery?"

Elsie gave a slow shake of her head.

"Good," Jason said. "Now. The last person you remember, I think, is the stage-door keeper. Right?"

"Yes. His name's Bill. Very sweet."

"You like him?"

"Oh, yes."

"Fine, Elsie, because we're going to help Bill by making him disappear. I want you to form a picture of him in your mind, please. All right? Good. Now destroy that picture. Have you done so?"

"Yes."

"Next, I want you to write on this blackboard, the one you can see in front of you, all the details you know of a doorman called Bill, a man whose face and form are not familiar to you. Write his full name, whether married or not, children, where he lives, his health. Understand?"

"Yes."

"Here is a piece of chalk. Write."

Elsie's hand came up confidently, the thumb and forefinger pincered, and began to make writing motions in the air before her face. It was another symptom of the profound trance, successful induction of hallucination.

When the actress lowered her arm, Jason said, "Take up the cloth and wipe the board clean. As you do so, all those facts will be wiped from your memory. Use the cloth, please."

Elsie again raised her hand, this time clawed. She made circular rubbing motions.

"Excellent," Jason said. "You're a good girl, Elsie. Would you like to rest for a while?"

"No, thank you." She spoke with the politeness of a child at someone else's party.

"In that case, let's talk about the last person you can recall—the stage manager. I want you to form a picture . . ."

● ● ● ● ● ●

The creative artist rarely knows the source of his ideas, his total plans for a particular work. He may think he does, or he may believe in that popular absurdity, inspiration, or he may consider himself privileged to receive favours from gods. In mundane point of truth, artistic concepts are experience.

The novelist, for example.

He is taken by a disturbing sensation at the age of three. At seven he witnesses a car accident and retains a vivid memory, not of the crash itself but of the appalling silence immediately afterwards. He sees a brutal fistfight at age twelve between two drunks. At sixteen he falls in love with a ballerina. Married, he watches the birth of his first child. At various times he is impressed by one scene in a motion picture or one simile in a book or the chime of colours in one painting. He sees, in passing, a derelict asleep in a doorway, a girl crying with happiness, a man being arrested, a funeral with a single mourner.

One day, a writer now, he gets an idea for a novel. It is presented to him whole. He thinks he has just invented it, but the source is his subconscious retention of past scenes and emotions; plus selections from film-book-painting, for all artists are innocent plagiarists.

So it was in a similar way with Jason Galt. He didn't know how or when he first got the idea for his plan. Could be it was while considering the privacy of his house. It might have been when he watched Jenny pay the rent out of her own earnings. The initial step may have been taken the day he met his ex-employer, the analyst, and heard, "You know, that patient, he never did come back."

And could be it was when casually reading a profile of Elsie Vanetti, the actress, he learned she had toured with a show whose top act was a hypnotist, and remembered, seeing the face again, that chorus girl who needed to stay away from the wings.

Whatever, Jason found one quiet evening that he had a complete scheme in his mind. He was intrigued and frightened and scoffing, and set about working mentally on the peripheral details of implementation.

The plot, he saw, had flaws. But they were small things, green spots of damp on a wall of pure white. The largest question mark hovered over himself, his ability. Was he good enough? Did he have the necessary skill?

Jason believed so. He presented his idea to Jenny:

Elsie Vanetti disappears. As she is famous, the newspapers of the world clamour. It's the sensation of the years. Dozens of theories are put forward. Its reputation on the block, Scotland Yard goes all out for a solution. Interpol is alerted, ports of exit are watched, the underworld is raked over. Every day the affair gets more mysterious, more sensational. Everyone is looking for Elsie Vanetti.

Just when interest is beginning to flag, the actress reappears. She is found wandering in the street. Her memory has gone. She remembers nothing of her past life; or possibly, with prodding, she recalls 10 per cent—names and faces and places which are meaningless to her out of lifetime context. As for the time since her disappearance, she has, she thinks, been simply wandering about.

Doctors are consulted. Eminent specialists fly in from various parts of the world. The affair is bigger than ever in the news media. And nothing happens. Elsie Vanetti fails to respond to treatment. She remembers nothing. The famous actress is a nonentity.

The final act features Jason Galt, a hypnotist. He asks to be allowed to try where others have failed. He tries, he succeeds. Overnight, the name of Jason Galt has international circulation.

Jenny's response was disappointing. The plan was not only criminal, she said, but impossible. Jason argued these into fragility.

"But you said yourself there were flaws," Jenny had complained.

"Mainly at the end, when everything else is over."

They were in the nearby park, ambling, both tense and alert. Jason spoke urgently. He had become wedded to his plan over the past days.

Avoiding mention of the doubt in his ability to destroy a subject's memory bank, his doubt in the possibility of this by any hypnotist, he said:

"There're two final risks. One, that they bring in a psychiatrist who uses hypnosis, and if so, that he's able to make her remember."

"Do you think he could?"

"I don't know. I doubt it. The controlling voice would be different, you see. And the second risk, that's if they suspect I might have entranced her in the first place. Suspect the whole scheme."

"They may not be able to prove it."

"And if they can't, if we take all necessary precautions, then I won't be hurt by suspicions."

"All right," Jenny said. "But before that, keeping her in the house. So many things could go wrong."

Again Jason held back his own misgivings. There was always the unexpected, the human element. But he was determined now to take his chances on the smaller risks.

He said, "One or the other of us would always be there. Nothing could happen."

"But what about . . ."

Jenny had dozens of questions, from sleeping arrangements to the sudden purchasing of extra food at the little store where they shopped. The questions were sound, as were Jason's answers.

Jenny lapsed into silence. She walked with her head down. Keeping abreast, Jason shot her nervous glances from time to time. At last he asked, "Well?"

She gave a fast lift-drop of her shoulders. "I don't know."

"Jen, it's important to me."

She moved close, took his arm and brought him to a stop. Looking up at him earnestly, she asked:

"Why? Why do you want to do this crazy thing?"

His answer was ready. "Fame and money," he said. "There are people of world renown in every field. There's no such animal as a famous hypnotist. I'd be it. The one and only. I could go to any country and pack theatres. It would change my whole life. There's nothing noble about it, Jen. I want fame and money. The ego trip in luxury."

"I see."

"And you'd have your share. If you'll help."

She spread her hands, sighing. "I don't know, Jason. I honestly don't."

Two days later, after a prolonged dialogue on the plan, Jenny agreed to help.

4

It was late afternoon. The traffic passed fast and dense along Bayswater Road, though it was heard only as a pale drone through the double-glazing of the Lancaster Gate flat.

Hull Rainer paced busily. One hand plucking at his bottom lip, stroking his chin and fiddling with his tie, he covered the whole flat —living room, hall, kitchen, bedrooms. He was waiting for the doorbell to ring.

Hull had lost his blasé jauntiness. There was no bounce in his walk. He looked like one of those grimly purposeful commuters who hustle from bus to subway.

His day had been harrowing. At eight he had started telephoning friends. Was Elsie there? Why no, she wasn't. He worked on through the list, getting down to mere acquaintances. No trace of Elsie.

At ten o'clock he started on the hospitals. None had admitted Miss Vanetti and there were no unidentified patients. Hull tried the producer of Elsie's play, who said he would check. He called back later: Elsie had left the theatre as usual. Hull telephoned the distant friends, in Scotland, Wales and Yorkshire, with negative results. As a last hope, he called his wife's mother, with whom Elsie was not on affectionate terms. Nothing, except complaints.

There was no avenue left other than the police. Hull called the local station. He talked with a sergeant, then a detective. An alert was sent out to all stations, hospitals were rechecked, enquiries were made at traffic divisions, private clinics and the offices of every international airline.

At four o'clock, two detectives came and took a statement. They also wanted photographs and a smooth-surface article handled recently by Elsie—Hull supplied a hairbrush.

Throughout these hours, whenever the telephone rang, Hull flung himself at it like a fool at folly. The caller was always a friend wanting news. Hull fumed and fretted. He worried lest Elsie be lying dead somewhere, he cursed her for an inconsiderate bitch.

Latest of all was a telephone message from the police. A Chief Inspector Wilkinson would be coming around shortly. That had been fifteen minutes ago.

Hull paced. He told himself that when Elsie did show up, she'd get the biggest chewing-out she'd ever had in her life, plus maybe a good smack across the face.

Sure, he thought, and then maybe Elsie would take a notion to break up the marriage—if she hadn't decided that already. Could she possibly have found out about some of his girls?

Hull was still considering this when the doorbell rang.

Chief Inspector Wilkinson looked to be in his mid-fifties. He had dense grey hair and a ruddy complexion. The pipe he held seemed somehow right. He had the flattened face of a boxer. It was impassive.

After introducing himself, in an accent which held the faint drawl of Devon or Cornwall, he said, "And this is Detective Sergeant Bart."

He stood to Wilkinson's rear, a tall, thin man of about thirty. He was bald and had a long, sad face with sleepy eyes. Both he and his superior wore the raincoats expected of the plain-clothes policeman.

Hull brought them inside. While everyone got settled, he talked about the weather, chattering. He was nervous. He didn't like it and avoided questioning its motive.

The detectives took a couch each. Hull sat on a third, facing the Chief Inspector. He offered cigarettes, coffee, drinks. All were politely declined.

Wilkinson said, "I expect you're pretty upset, sir."

"Of course. Terribly upset. I can't imagine what it's all about. It's the not knowing."

"Exactly, sir. I know how it is. Our little girl went missing once, years ago, and we were frantic. You have children?"

The question, coming unexpectedly, made Hull stare. He said, "Er —no. No children. That's for later."

Wilkinson puffed his pipe for a moment before saying, "Well now, Mr Rainer, what I'm going to do first is list the possible reasons for your wife's disappearance. Okay?"

"Yes."

"An accident seems to be ruled out. Unless, of course, it was a hit-

and-run job and the driver's hidden the body. That's happened before."

Hull cleared his throat unhappily. "Yes."

"Next," Wilkinson said, "comes suicide."

"I think we can rule that out as well."

"Your wife was happy, sir? Her state of mind was good?"

"Elsie's in fine shape," Hull said emphatically. "Home and career—great. She has no cause to do anything like that. Besides, she would have been found."

The Chief Inspector rocked his head gently, as if slipping punches. "There's the river. Or she could have done it in some secluded spot."

"No. Suicide, no."

"Okay, let's move on. What comes next, Bart?"

The sleepy-sad man said, addressing Hull, "We thought, sir, that the most obvious answer would be that she's left home."

"Without a word, a note?" Hull asked. "Not Elsie. She's not like that. In any case, our relationship is sound. Never better. And there's the play. She wouldn't walk out, leaving everyone in the lurch."

Wilkinson looked at his wristwatch. "She might show up at the theatre for tonight's performance, of course."

"I suppose."

"In fact, shall we agree to use that as a yardstick, Mr Rainer? Shall we say that if she fails to appear there, it will mean she's definitely missing, we start a full-scale search and inform the press?"

"Yes," Hull said. "I guess that's sensible." His head was beginning to ache. He wished he had never informed the police. That Elsie might show up at the theatre seemed to him now most likely. He would be made to look a fool.

Chief Inspector Wilkinson said, his eyes watchful, "One aspect we, the CID, have to consider, is that this could be a hoax."

"Hoax?"

"For publicity, Mr Rainer."

Irritated, Hull said, "My wife couldn't be more famous if she tried. Believe me, she doesn't need publicity. She's not a movie glamour queen, she's a serious actress. Why, she doesn't even employ a press agent."

Wilkinson appeared satisfied. This showed in his manner; there was no change in his flat features. He put a match to his pipe, watched calmly by the other man, impatiently by Hull.

Blowing out smoke, the Inspector said, "Could have been kidnapped."

Hull swallowed a sigh. This was all so stupid and unnecessary, he thought. But he mustn't appear too complacent.

He said, "That is a vague possibility, I imagine."

"Are you and your wife well off financially, sir?"

"Reasonably so. Not rich. Few are in the acting profession."

"Seems to me I read that Miss Vanetti got half a million dollars for working in that big picture a while back."

"She did. But there was a large tax bite, not to mention agency fees and a hundred other little expenses."

"The public, though. I dare say they think of you as rich people."

"I dare say."

"So. A couple of villains snatch Miss Vanetti, take her to a hideout, and then make contact with you with a ransom demand."

"Sounds a bit melodramatic, Inspector."

"Crime always is, Mr Rainer."

Hull said, "Anyway, the kidnappers would have been in touch by now, surely."

"There's no hurry."

Detective Sergeant Bart said, "They could be using the post to make contact."

Wilkinson nodded. "Quite so."

Hull asked, "You really think she could have been kidnapped?"

"It's a distinct possibility, sir. One we should prepare for. If you get an extortion letter, be careful how you handle it. Should contact be made by phone, we'd like your permission to put a tap on the instrument."

"That's fine," Hull said, dismal. He was seeing a picture of himself handing over a large sum of money for Elsie's return. It sickened him.

He felt worse when next the Inspector spoke. The words caused in him an aching hollowness in the diaphragm. It was like the sensation you get from seeing a running child suddenly fall.

"Last on the list," Wilkinson said, "is murder."

Hull took a long, slow breath to steady himself. He shook his head. "That's ridiculous."

"Tragic and terrible, sir, but not ridiculous."

"I meant the idea. Elsie. Who would murder Elsie?"

The Inspector peered into the bowl of his pipe. "To begin with, a stranger. Mugger, rapist, maniac. He, like our hit-and-run driver, takes away the evidence and hides it."

"Well . . . ," Hull said reluctantly.

"After that," Wilkinson said, looking up, "we have murder by person or persons known. Known to the victim, that is. And sooner or later to us."

"Inspector. No one would have a reason for killing my wife."

"Oh, there's always a motive," Wilkinson said, impassive as ever. "In the case of Miss Vanetti, it could be professional. A rival, perhaps. Or her understudy getting desperate."

Hull forced a laugh. "Theatrical rivals don't murder. And Elsie's understudy, she wouldn't hurt a mouse."

"It would need going into, of course. I know nothing about the acting world. Seems to me, though, that emotions run pretty high with you people."

Hull shrugged. "All bluster."

"Next," Wilkinson said, "there's private life. I'd like to ask you, Mr Rainer, if you don't mind, if your wife had any attachments outside marriage."

Hull asked coldly, "Do you mean lovers?"

"Yes."

"She has no lovers. My wife is a highly moral person. Which is not all that rare in the theatre, despite what people think."

"I see."

"And I'd appreciate it, Inspector, if you wouldn't refer to my wife in the past tense."

Wilkinson slipped invisible punches again. "I'll try to remember that, sir," he said. "Sorry." Surprisingly, he sounded as if he meant it. Which made his next question all the harsher.

He asked, "Do you have a mistress, Mr Rainer?"

Stiffly: "I beg your pardon?"

"Routine question, sir. Don't be offended. I need to know about people who might want your wife out of the way."

"I do not have a mistress, Inspector. I have never had a mistress. I do not intend to have a mistress. Does that answer your routine question?"

For a brief moment, Wilkinson's face lost its impassivity. The expression which came and went, however, was defiant to definition except for what seemed to Hull to be a taste for brutality.

The Inspector put his pipe away. He leaned forward, clasped pudgy hands on one knee and said:

"That leaves us with murder for profit. Monetary gain. Could you tell me, please, if Miss Vanetti has made a will."

"She has. So have I. We've each named the other as sole beneficiary."

"I see."

Lightly, Hull asked, "Would that make me a suspect?"

"Anything's possible, Mr Rainer."

Hull felt himself redden. Absurdly, he felt guilty. He snapped out an unconvincing, "What nonsense."

Wilkinson asked calmly, "Should it be required, sir, would you be able to account for your movements last night?"

"An alibi?"

"Exactly, sir. An alibi."

"Yes, as it happens, I could account for my movements. Every minute between nine and midnight."

"Good. Would you mind telling me where you were?"

"Inspector," Hull said, as if with resignation. "I think you're being a little premature. These questions are silly when my wife might come walking in at any moment. But if it's worth anything to you, I'll confess to the fact that I have not murdered my wife."

"Fine. And your alibi?"

"Should it be required, you said. Let's wait till that time, Inspector."

Hull stood up. "Now, if you'll excuse me, I have to go out."

"Well, sir, I was going to ask if you'd mind if we had a look around the flat here."

"I *would* mind. My wife is not here. There's no sense in wasting time. I'm going out to look for Elsie. *You* might try it as well." He looked pointedly from man to man. "*If* you'll excuse me?"

● ● ● ● ● ●

Five minutes later, alone, Hull poured himself a four-finger whisky. His hand was unsteady. Noting the tremor made him feel worse. He was badly shaken. He began to see where Elsie's disappearance might lead.

Suppose, he thought, she had been killed in some way, or had thrown herself in the river, or had taken off and gone into permanent hiding. Wilkinson might follow up his suspicions. He could say it was for the money, or professional jealousy, or sheer hate. All untrue, of course, but cops had nasty minds. They might even be able to prove he did it.

Hull drank off the whisky. He strode around the living room. The silence worked on the edges of his fraying nerves. He began to feel trapped.

Leaving the flat, he went downstairs and out to the street. He started to walk quickly. It was only when he saw a telephone booth that he remembered his alibi.

Gasping, he went inside and got the slip of paper from his sock. He fed the coin slot and dialled. The call signal ended, a lilting voice said:

"Nan Mountford. Hello."

A good sign, Hull felt. She was at home and he now knew her name.

"Nan darling," he said. "This is Hull. Did you find my note this morning?"

"Oh, Hull," the girl said, sounding pleased. "How lovely of you to ring. Yes, I got the note. Sorry you had to charge off. I'd rather thought we might have breakfast out and the drive . . ."

She rattled on. Making suitable remarks, Hull forced himself to patience. It wouldn't do, he thought, to sound flustered. He was, in any case, beginning to find calm.

Nan Mountford slowing at last, Hull said, "By the way, darling, something quite odd has happened. Hilarious really, but it could be rather awkward. Listen."

He gave her the whole story, making it light. Three times the girl interrupted, and with each one her voice lost a shade more of its lilt. She said, "I didn't know you were married," and, "Disappeared?" and, "The police asked what?"

Hull finished, "So there you are. If they insist, I guess I'll have to say I was at your place and—"

"Don't you dare!" the girl said, her voice a yap without music. "You just keep me out of it. It's none of my business. Daddy would be furious. I'll deny it. I'll deny ever meeting you. Don't ring me again. Go away. I want nothing more to do with you."

A violent click sounded in the receiver. Hull cradled it wearily. He pushed his way out of the booth and walked on. His tension had been replaced by a tired wretchedness.

He realised that even if he did persuade Nan Mountford to co-operate, the police might think the story had been concocted, or, worse, would conclude that he was not the loving, faithful husband he had claimed.

Hull trudged on, head down and hands deep in his pockets.

Abruptly he thought of home. Elsie might have come back. She could be sitting there waiting, with a fantastic story of some kind to explain the mystery. She might be making tea and singing and wearing her old robe with the necktie girdle.

A lump of fondness for his wife swelled in Hull's throat. He moved forward into a run. Not until he reached the building did he slow.

When approaching the door of his flat, he heard ringing inside. He hurried in and over to the telephone. The caller was the producer of Elsie's play.

He said, "I've rung you four times."

"Went out."

"Any news?"

Hull covered the mouthpiece to call, "Elsie!" There was no answer. He took his hand away. "No news. You?"

"No. Curtain-up in ten minutes. The understudy's going on. What the hell is Elsie playing at?"

Hull droned, "I wish to God I knew."

"There's two bloody great policemen here."

"Wilkinson and Bart, I suppose."

The producer unwound a string of obscenities before the coherence of, "Making bloody nuisances of themselves. Asking questions, getting in the way. How long is this going to go on?"

"She'll show up, Roger. Don't worry about it."

"Hope so. Got to go. Keep in touch. Bye."

Hull walked unsteadily from the telephone table to a couch. He let himself sprawl and stared gauntly at the ceiling. This, he thought, is the worst thing that's ever happened to me in my life.

PART TWO

5

The morning was fine and bright, like a promise. Smiling as they walked, early commuters shot grateful glances up at the sun. Housewives opened windows, shopkeepers propped back their doors to give a gaping welcome. Like hounds after feeding, the city-bound traffic had lost much of its snarl.

Jason Galt strolled. He felt tranquil. There was an expression almost of whimsy on his handsome face. He had left off his windcheater in order to feel the perky morning chill, in order to know that he was outdoors.

Ahead in the row of businesses, Jason could see his goal, a newspaper shop. He had a glow of expectation; it waxed all the friendlier for his knowing there was no chance of disappointment. The story had broken.

Last night on television, at ten and again at midnight, the newscaster had followed two political events with:

"It has been announced by New Scotland Yard that the well-known actress Elsie Vanetti is missing from home. She has not been seen since eleven last night. Her role in the West End play in which she is currently appearing was acted this evening by an understudy. A police spokesman said no further statement would be made at this time, but asked that members of the public who might have pertinent information contact their local police stations."

Brief and lacking frills, the item was obviously a mere preliminary, Jason had thought. A preparation. After all, she had been gone only twenty-four hours, and the item itself could well suffice to bring her back. The big hue and cry would follow.

Jason had resisted playing his radio this morning. He wanted to read his notices, not hear them, or even have them with visual effects on TV. In common with most people, Jason was convinced only by the printed word. To be sure, to be satisfied in his emotional being, he needed that often meaningless entity, "something in writing."

He drew nearer to his goal. He could see the headlines of the racked newspapers outside, first the screamers and then the sedate. His glow thrived.

Stopping by the rack, he looked at every banner. The missing actress got top place except in the *Guardian*. He smiled in congratulation at the *Sun*'s VEEP VANETTI VANISHES.

Inside the shop he bought three papers. *Telegraph* for veracity and exhaustive reporting, *Express* for the middle slant, *Mirror* for colour and hyperbole. He bought with acted indifference, even though the woman spared him merely a glance.

Out on the street again, papers under his arm, Jason continued his walk and his glow. It felt good simply to be out of the house and moving.

The day before, Jason had worked with Elsie right through to ten o'clock. It was the confinement he had found enervating, whereas he had expected the work itself to bring him low with its tedium. Instead, the long hours of murmuring voices, Elsie's and his own, had given him an unusual sensation of peace. It had puzzled him slightly. It puzzled him still.

Between news telecasts, Jason had been obliged to read for the third time, making notes, a biography of Elsie Vanetti. The paperback original was full of details which would be useful. After midnight he had shuffled through the Vanetti interviews he had recently clipped from periodicals, and spent some time on the soles of Elsie's shoes. The walk he would have enjoyed at one in the morning, he had to forego: there was the risk of being stopped and questioned by police on car patrol: such small incidents could have large consequences.

Walking faster, eager now, Jason soon came to a cafe. It was clean inside despite its exuded stench of stale food fried in exhausted grease. The customers were mostly uniformed men from the nearby bus depot.

Before going to a table, Jason stopped at the counter to order bacon and eggs. Elsie, whom he had brought from sleep to a light trance, would be having the same with Jenny. It pleased him somehow, knowing that.

He began to read. His glow settling nicely, he read during and after the meal and through a second cup of coffee. Once he winced, this at *The actress is married to Hull Rainer, an actor*. Being *an* rather than *the* made the man a no one. Jason's wince was out of sympathy.

There were no theories as to the why of Elsie Vanetti's disappearance. That would come later, the news itself digested. In the main, the papers stuck to background and career. They reported that ports of exit were being watched, underworld contacts were being questioned, a large group of officers had been put on the case under the supervision of a Chief Inspector Harold Wilkinson.

There were photographs. The *Telegraph* had front and profile publicity shots. The *Express* had something similar plus a view of the theatre. The *Mirror* had two close-ups, a picture of the block of flats where the actress lived and one of her as a leggy chorus girl.

All three papers carried the same mock-up supplied by New Scotland Yard, along with details of colouring. The last-seen-wearing picture was the head of Elsie Vanetti on the body of a model in a raincoat and flat shoes; a police artist had added sunglasses and a headscarf.

An additional fact was that the actress had been carrying a purse. Of dark-blue leather, its contents included, it was believed, an Equity card bearing Miss Vanetti's name.

Jason leaned back with a sigh. He was mightily satisfied. Often while planning the scheme he had imagined himself reading the newspapers, seeing what he had accomplished in all its blaring, sensational glory. Realisation was not disappointing.

He closed his eyes. This was a happy moment. He would have liked to tell someone about it. Ownership needs to be known about before pride of it can reach full blossom. Jason sighed again.

He got up and went over to the counter to pay. When handing back his change, the woman, darkly Mediterranean, nodded at the newspapers he carried and said:

"How about that, then? The actress."

Jason smiled. "They're making a big noise about it."

"Big name. Elsie Vanetti."

"Yes, I believe she's quite famous," Jason said. He felt marvellous.

The woman narrowed her eyes. "Know what I reckon?"

"No."

"I reckon she's done a bunk. Bet you she owes money all over the place. These fillum stars."

"She looks very nice, though. Respectable."

"Yeh, but she's not English, see."

"Italian," Jason said. "I suppose."

Pulling a scornful face, the woman said, "Eyetalian me foot. She's Sicilian. Odd lot, they are. Dangerous."

"Oh, well."

The woman turned away to another customer. Jason left. Smiling, he set off for home.

● ● ● ● ● ●

He closed the front door loudly and called, "Hello!"

Above, feet pattered a tattoo. Next, Jenny appeared at the stairhead, plate and dishcloth in hand. She asked breathlessly, "Yes?"

"Yes and double yes. They're full of it."

"Come on up. Quick." Like Jason, Jenny had to read to believe.

They spent the following minutes with the newspapers. Jenny was grinningly nervous, Jason like a boy showing off a new acquisition. He re-read every word.

Sated, he straightened from the table and looked around. "Elsie's back in her room?"

Still engrossed, Jenny mumbled, "That's right."

"Did she eat well?"

"Yes."

Jason stepped to the breakfront. From a drawer he got a brown-paper parcel, took it to the couch and sat down. He unwrapped the paper, revealing a purse of blue leather.

As he slipped open the catch, Jason had a curious sensation. It made him pause. The feeling seemed to be part embarrassment, part self-censure, and part unknown.

All of it, he told himself sternly, was foolish. Normally he wouldn't go nosing through someone's personal belongings, no, but this was essential to the plan. Or anyway, if not essential, something that should be done.

It occurred to Jason, with a wry smile, that his defence was as stupid as the emotional objection. What was personal property compared to interference with a life, someone's freedom?

And that, he mused, was the kind of thinking he had to avoid.

He opened the mouth of the purse wide and began to take out the articles one at a time. There were nail-file and clippers, three ball-point pens, a bunch of keys, a lipstick, a small pack of tissues, a steel letter-opener engraved with THIS IS TO USE ON YOUR FIRST-NIGHT CABLES. There was eight pounds and fifty pence. And there was the Equity card.

Jason smiled at the last. It was going to make things easier.

"Aren't you forgetting something?"

He looked up. Jenny, by the table, was watching him. He asked, "What?"

"Fingerprints."

"I haven't forgotten. I'll see to it now."

Jenny nodded absently. Glancing behind her at the strewn newspapers, she said, "They don't mention any possible reasons. Her disappearance."

"They'll get around to it."

"I wonder what the police're thinking."

"God knows."

"What if someone comes up with the idea that she's lost her memory?"

"It's a long shot," Jason said. With his handkerchief he was wiping each article before he put it back in the purse. Some he wiped only on the part where they had been carefully picked up; he didn't want the contents to be totally clean, therefore patently wiped.

He added, "If anyone does get that idea, it won't make much difference."

They were silent for a moment. Jenny said, "I let Elsie wash her face. I hope that's all right." Her tone was faintly on the offensive.

"Sure."

"I left her hair."

"Good."

"But listen," Jenny said. "Listen dear." Her voice had switched to the warmth of persuasion.

"Well?" Jason asked warily.

"The poor girl needs a bath. She's itchy and uncomfortable. She hasn't been out of those clothes for ages."

"It's not that long."

"Ages, Jason. It won't make that much difference at this point. Won't you let her have a bath?"

Jason closed the purse and wrapped it in the paper. "Sorry," he said. "For this to work, all the details have to be right. No more face washing either."

Jenny sighed, shrugged, turned away. She swung around to say, "Well, at least let her take that damn coat off."

Jason shook his head. "Sorry." He got up and put the parcel back in the drawer. "And thanks for reminding me about that coat."

"You're being very difficult."

He held out an appealing hand. "Please, dear. Don't keep making it harder for me."

She turned away again.

Jason looked at his watch. "I'd better get to work. Take a break, if you like. Go out."

"All right. We need groceries anyway."

"See you later," Jason said. He went into the back bedroom.

Elsie Vanetti was sitting on the upright chair. She stared lazily straight ahead. Her hair was a straggly mess, her coat crumpled. Yet she looked far from unattractive, Jason thought. She looked like a country girl, tired from a hike in the wind.

He set about deepening her trance. This he was now able to accomplish in two minutes, their rapport strong, and growing stronger. He could see the time when with a few words he would be able to shift her hypnoidal state from light to profound or back again.

He said, "Stand up, Elsie."

She rose obediently.

"I want you to lie in the grass, this lovely green grass. I want you to enjoy it, roll on it. Lie down, please."

Elsie lowered herself to the threadbare carpet. She stretched out flat. Awkwardly, she began to roll. When stopped by the wall, she rolled back.

"You liked that," Jason told her. "Now get up, please, and sit on your chair."

Jason went to the bed. He felt vaguely disgruntled with himself, which, he imagined, must be because he had been reminded of Jenny's nagging.

Stretching out on the bed, he looked at the ceiling and said, "Elsie, I am giving you a flower. Here. Take it in your left hand. All right?"

"Yes."

"With your right hand I want you to crush the bloom. Go ahead. Crush it. Have you done that?"

There was no answer. Jason looked around.

Elsie's hands were held in front of her, one above the other, left clenched, right clawed—clawed and trembling. Her face was troubled.

Jason asked, "What is it, Elsie? Why are you hesitating?"

She said, clumsily, as if the words were ejected lumps of fat, "I don't want to hurt the flower."

Jason had again that sensation he had experienced when opening the purse. He thrust it aside and sat up.

"It is not a flower, Elsie. It is a nettle. You have to grasp it tight or it will sting. Is that not right?"

"Yes."

"Grasp the nettle."

Her right hand made a convulsive snatching motion, while her lips firmed with determination.

Jason was satisfied. He could have made her crush the non-existent flower, but it wasn't necessary. There was no need to press the unimportant.

After he had deepened Elsie's trance still further, he took a page of notes from the hip pocket of his jeans and lay back on the bed. He began the session of question and answer, order and obedience.

Jason had already obliterated much from Elsie Vanetti's memory —the play and all those connected with it, her apartment and cleaning woman, her husband's name and appearance. But there were hundreds of details which would remind her of these and which might cancel the superficial amnesia. The still-kept memory of dozens of discussions with her dresser, say, might bring the woman herself back into focus when seen face to face. The same with others, especially the husband.

Therefore, Jason had decided against a strict procedure of working backwards in time. With his notes and what he garnered from Elsie's answers, he would hunt and destroy across the whole landscape of her life.

Time passed.

Jason felt at his ease. He was confident of gaining his 90 per cent success. He knew, for instance, that Elsie's description of her home would not be absolutely accurate, that once back there she would recognise some item which she had not mentioned and which might strike through the blanket order to forget the whole place; but that was an unavoidable segment of the 10 per cent.

Constantly Jason asked, "Does that remind you of something that happened later, maybe years afterwards?" And, "Had you ever met that person before?" And, "Can you recall other outings like that?" And, "Did you ever go back?"

He jumped from a kindergarten teacher to the doctor she had seen last year; from a weekend cottage in the Lake District to a pre-marriage flat in Ealing; from a politician who looked like a friend to the landlord of her local pub; from a garden party at Buckingham Palace to a semi-orgy in Hollywood; from a magnificent Broadway theatre to a jaded music hall in the English provinces.

"Who was the star of that show, Elsie?"

"A hypnotist."

"His name?"

"Gilt. Galt. James Galt. I think that's it."

"Can you recall his face?"

"A little. Dimly."

"Forget him. Forget the theatre. Forget the word hypnotism."

He talked on, covering the whole show and her particular friend of that time.

He asked, "There's a blank period there, right?"

"Yes."

"And next, you were nineteen years old."

"Yes."

More out of curiosity than endeavour, Jason asked, "What was your ambition at that time?"

"What it's always been."

"Tell me."

Elsie smiled quietly. Her eyes, on Jason, looked wistful. "All I've ever wanted," she said, "was to be happy."

●●●●●●

The early promise had held good, like an agreement between innocents. The day was warm and keen clear. In the City, London's financial district, the narrow streets were aswarm with lunchtime escapers from bank and office and shop.

The steps of St Paul's Cathedral were so packed with sitting people, some with sandwiches, that the pigeons were forced onto the pavement. They squabbled there irritably like delegates at a peace conference.

Jason moved along at a casual stroll. He was in no hurry. Furthermore, he wanted this to be done with care and perfection. He had made, he felt, a good start.

His choice of clothing had been right. That was obvious now, here. Had he worn the old coat and hat, he would have been noticeable as much for the outfit's shabby state as for its inappropriateness to the weather.

Jason was in his best suit, a single-breasted grey flannel. His shirt was white, the tie sober. He had oiled his hair and combed it flat. He looked no different from those among whom he walked; and the package under his arm might have been sandwiches.

However: he did have a minor fret. Sometime soon, a matter of weeks, his face would become known to the public—hopefully. Would anyone from this noon, therefore, place that face with the man possibly noticed today?

Jason thought not. The odds were extremely long against such a contingency. But, in respect of being noticed, the dropping place had to be selected with deliberation.

He came to a tavern, entered the vestibule and eased open the door. The noise that came out in attack was enough to tell him the place was crowded. Fine for anonymity, bad for the other part of it.

Jason walked on. That, he thought, the other part, was where the main problem lay. There was no guarantee of success. He had no power over the finder.

It was for that reason, more than personal safety, that Jason had decided against what he knew to be more suitable to his cause, to the affair in its continuing newsworthiness—the bizarre, the romantic, the sinister.

He would have preferred as a dropping place somewhere like the Tower of London, the middle of Westminster Bridge, a seat on a fairground's giant wheel, or a gambling club in Chinatown. Unfortunately, it just wasn't feasible.

Jason passed a cafeteria. He turned, went back and looked through the window, looking beyond the shelves of cakes and tarts. The room was deep. It had three lines of tables running back from the window display. Parallel was the long counter. Both it and the tables had a medium quota of customers.

Jason liked the attributes. What especially took his fancy was the fact that the nearest table, first of the centre line, was vacant, and that where he stood now would make an excellent observation post.

He went in.

At the counter, not taking a tray, Jason moved past those waiting to be served main courses, past the ponderers over desserts, and past the selectors of cellophane-wrapped snacks.

He stopped beside a couple at the drinks section.

There was a leaning stack of paper napkins. Jason noticed it as he was reaching in a pocket for his handkerchief. A napkin would look much better, so natural as to be unnoticeable. He took one.

The couple moved. Behind the counter, a youth with acne chanted, "Coffee, tea, milk?"

"Coffee, please. Black."

The youth poured, slid over cup and saucer, turned to the next person. "Coffee, tea, milk?"

With the napkin covering thumb and forefinger, Jason picked up the saucer. He moved on.

At the cash desk, a woman watched his approach. She was fat and surly-eyed and middle-aged. Her eyes threw hate at Jason's cup, then loathing at his face, then disgust at the package under his arm.

Jason prickled with heat. His heart began a gentle tapping. He realised his mistake. To take up table space with a mere drink when it was the busy lunch hour, that was bad enough; to bring what could be sandwiches, that was next to illegal.

Jason reached the desk. Awkwardly he transferred the cup to his left hand and with the other fumbled for change. He asked, "How much?"

The woman looked away. "Price board's in front of you," she rasped. "Sir."

Jason located the price. He put down the right sum and glanced at the woman. She was still looking away. Her unpleasant gaze was on the tray of an approaching customer, adding figures.

Jason went on.

He was not eased by the cashier's lack of further interest. His error had shaken him badly. And he saw now that his chosen table had been taken.

There were no others available. He began to move along an aisle. He felt grossly large. His confidence gone, he shuffled past a Negress who was putting dishes onto a metal cart.

The tap of Jason's heart was stronger. What if he had to go on pacing the aisles? he thought. People would be sure to notice. They'd stare, remember, and later recognise. Best to put the cup down and leave and . . .

The corner table, next to his own: people were leaving it.

Jason hurried forward.

Even before the last person turned away, Jason had sat at the table. He put his drink among the dirty plates, clasped his hands between his knees and looked down.

The pose fitted his spirits. He was unnerved by the mistake he had made. Other possibilities of error came into his mind. He began to see the whole affair from a new angle, one of derision.

It was a vast absurdity, he fumed. It was a juvenile idea. Crazy.

Wild. Even the hope of destroying Elsie's memory, that part alone, was a stupidity born of a sick ego. He should call the scheme off at once. Go home and release his prisoner. His victim.

Jason sat on in gloomy reverie, yet calming, until he was roused by a clatter of dishes. He looked up. The Negress was approaching with her cart.

It was now or not at all.

Jason glanced around. No one was paying him attention. His hands hidden from view by the table, he unwrapped the parcel and up-ended it over the next chair, depositing the purse there. The paper he flattened and slid inside his jacket.

He got up. With a hand rubbing the side of his face, he sidled like a servant to the door, and out.

Still dreary, confident only of failure, he stood by the window and looked beyond the shelves. The Negress was almost at the corner table now.

Jason questioned: Would she miss the purse? Would she tuck it inside her smock and keep it for herself?

A girl moved in front of Jason's view. She was looking back, talking to someone by the counter. She turned on reaching the corner table.

Jason held his breath.

About to sit down, the girl paused. She had seen the purse. After looking about, she picked it up and went to the Negress, thrust it into her hands, spoke, came back to the table.

Jason breathed again. He recovered to the point where he was able to remind himself that his position here by the window was quite ordinary, not suspicious-seeming.

The Negress was as casual about the purse as had been the finder. Such things, Jason realised, must of course happen every day. He had vaguely been expecting excitement, a bustle.

The Negress left her cart. She went to the cash desk, put down the purse and left.

Jason changed position to get a better view.

The cashier was busy with a customer. Alone again, she lifted the purse, opened it and fingered the contents. Another customer came, the purse was put aside. There were three more customers.

Jason clenched his fists.

The woman at the cash desk went back to the purse. She rooted inside, brought out a card, peered at it closely.

Her mouth opened wide, as if for its tongue to be spooned. Following a series of blinks, her eyes took on a look of delight Jason would never have thought them capable of.

The woman quickly left her seat.

Jason strode away.

● ● ● ● ● ●

Fifteen minutes later, Jason had recovered completely from his attack of nerves and his dismay at the project in hand. He had, indeed, almost forgotten his session of doubt. His sureness had come back.

He was leaning on the side of a tea-wagon, a trundly stall on wheels which held a gutter position in a street-market. The decrepit area lay a five-minute walk from the Bank of England.

Jason held a mug of tea lovingly. He fingered it with perverse pleasure. He was pleased with himself.

The only thing missing, Jason thought, was someone to tell with gentle brag of what he had accomplished. It was the sharing everyone needed.

As he sipped his tea, blinking at the steam, into Jason's mind came Elsie Vanetti. He evoked her face. With clarity he saw that serene forehead, the broad mouth with its full lower lip, those large dark eyes, the outcurving nose. He heard her voice, soft yet with an underlying throb of vitality; and allowed it to say things he remembered.

Yes, he thought, straightening and looking at his watch. It was time to get back to work.

6

Hull Rainer went down the service stairway of his apartment building. Since he was sure there were reporters at the entrance, he thought there might even be some in the lobby. Hull was not in the mood for reporters.

He had lost his smoothness of appearance. His hair was untidy, his clothes sat on him like those of a successful dieter, he had cut himself shaving, marks of tiredness roved his face.

Whereas Hull normally descended stairs briskly, erectly, arms loose at his sides (the entrance-maker), he now moved as if with caution, as if afraid of falling.

He passed the door which led to the lobby and went down one last flight. Circumspectly he entered the underground garage. There was no one around. He got in his sports car, started it, drove away.

As Hull came off the top of the ramp, he swung his gaze first to see whether the street was clear for him to pull out, second to see if he had been right about journalists.

He had. Half a dozen men were lounging by the entrance. They looked around sharply. One raised a camera.

Turning his car in the opposite direction, Hull roared off with racketing tyres. He changed gear viciously.

The press interest caused him to feel uneasy, even slightly nauseous. One or two men would have been fairly acceptable. But a group? Was interest so strong in the *husband?*

Hull slowed to light a cigarette. The smoke tasted acrid in his mouth, which already had the flavour of charcoal. It was an additional depressant to Hull that the present circumstances of threat had upgraded him as a smoker from moderate to chain.

Turning his head to the side, he spat away the new lit cigarette.

As for the ungentle bastards of the press, he thought, they could be there simply in the hopes of Elsie turning up. But that was getting more remote by the hour.

There had been no news. No word or sign. The half-expected ransom letter had not arrived. The telephone calls had been from friends, from newspapers, from a crackpot who claimed to have made Elsie vanish with magic, from the char writing to know if she should come in as usual—Hull said no—and from Chief Inspector Wilkinson with the request that Hull call to see him at the local station.

"Why?" Hull had asked.

"Just a little chat, Mr Rainer."

"Third-degree? Truncheons and bright lights?"

"Really, sir."

"Has there been a break?"

"Afraid not. Will you come round?"

"Okay. Later."

The journey took four minutes. Hull parked his car before the new building in a space that said it was reserved for the police surgeon. Hull felt a mite lifted by his cheek. I'm down but not out, he thought.

Inside the building, Hull stood uncertainly among the large room's bustle. People milled, a child was crying, clatter came from typewriters and from shoes on the tile floor.

At Hull's side appeared a constable. He asked, "Mr Rainer?"

"Yes."

"This way, please."

Chief Inspector Wilkinson was in a small room with an oversize desk. Apart from straight chairs, there was no other furniture, no piece of usual office equipment. The bareness Wilkinson explained, after inviting Hull to sit, with:

"This is HQ for the Vanetti case. The local boys have put it at my disposal."

Rudely, Hull asked, "Why did you want to see me?"

The flat face showed no emotion. Its owner shuffled papers, found his pipe and said, "I've been talking to friends and colleagues of your wife, Mr Rainer."

"And?"

"Yesterday, last night and this morning. I've seen quite a few people. Nearly all of them mentioned something I failed to get from you. Perhaps you forgot."

Hull didn't know what he was talking about. He brought out cigarettes, lit one, waited.

Wilkinson said, "I'm referring to Miss Vanetti's behaviour."

Hull blew out smoke, waited.

"Do I have your interest, Mr Rainer?"

"In what, Inspector?"

"Your wife," Wilkinson said. "She has been acting oddly these past few weeks."

"You learn something new every day."

A long stare, and, "You mean everyone else noticed it and you didn't?"

"I know nothing whatever about everyone else. I only know about me."

"Your wife seemed perfectly normal?"

"Perfectly."

Wilkinson put a match to his pipe. Between puffs he said, "Very curious."

Hull managed to hide his irritation. He would have liked to continue his waiting routine, but was compelled to ask:

"What was wrong with her behaviour?"

"It was odd, Mr Rainer. She had changed. A different woman, was the way it was put by more than one person. She had periods of depression. Twice backstage she flared up with her colleagues, which was unlike her. Sometimes she wouldn't answer when spoken to. Her dresser found her in tears on several occasions. You knew none of this?"

Hull shook his head. "It doesn't amaze me, though," he said. "First of all, her role in the play was very intense. Second, people exaggerate."

"Not all of them, surely. Tears? Arguments? You can't exaggerate those. They happened. And you explain them with her role."

"It's a suggestion."

"Then, she should have cried at home, argued with you."

"Inspector," Hull said, "home is sanctuary. Elsie is rarely touched there by her professional life."

"Frankly, Mr Rainer, I don't share your casual attitude. The behaviour of Miss Vanetti seems to me to be that of a person under great strain."

"All right. Maybe. And maybe she was hiding it from me. If so, what would it mean?"

Wilkinson looked up at his pipe. He said, "Could be she felt menaced."

"I don't know by what."

"Or by whom?"

"No."

"Possibly," the Inspector said, "she was being blackmailed."

Hull sighed. He said in a droning voice, "We have a joint bank account. She couldn't get anything out without my knowing. Her jewellery is at the flat—I've been through all her things. I doubt if she was being blackmailed."

"She may not have paid yet."

"Have it your own way."

"Mr Rainer, can you offer another way, a theory for her odd actions, apart from the play?"

Hull stubbed out his cigarette. "She may have found out she was sick. Really ill. She may have been heading for a nervous breakdown. Either of which could also explain her disappearance. She's gone into a clinic, under another name."

"Any history of nervous breakdowns?"

"No."

"Well," the Inspector said, "I prefer my own theories."

"You do seem to have a fondness for the dramatic."

Unperturbed, Wilkinson said, "Which reminds me. A Charles Wheldon of UK-TV telephoned me about the case. He wondered if it might help if you were to appear on television, make a sort of appeal."

"I shouldn't think so," Hull said, shrugging.

"You do believe, don't you, that your wife is still alive?"

"I don't know what to believe. I'm hoping."

Unexpectedly, Wilkinson asked, "How's your alibi?"

"Very well, thanks. Waiting to be needed."

"That could be very soon."

"Also, it could not," Hull said. "I'll give Charles Wheldon a ring."

"Good."

"Is there anything else before I go?"

The inspector said, "Just one item, Mr Rainer. We found your wife's purse."

Hull had been midway to his feet. He sat again heavily. "You found what?"

"Miss Vanetti's purse. An hour ago. In a cafeteria in the City."

Hull flared, "Why the hell didn't you say so before?"

Wilkinson went so far as to raise his eyebrows. "I wanted to discuss the more interesting matter of your wife's behaviour."

"Thought I might fall in a heap and confess to doing her in?"

"One never knows."

Evenly, Hull said, "Chief Inspector Harold Wilkinson is a bit of a pig."

"He's a man doing his job."

Hull sneered. He asked, "Where's the purse?"

"In the lab. Prints. There's no lead on your wife in the cafeteria. Not so far. We're working on it."

"Okay," Hull said, leaning forward. "So what does the purse mean? Was Elsie there? or did someone else leave it?"

"At the moment we don't know. There's money in it, which is curious."

"Mysteriouser and mysteriouser."

The Inspector smiled. He actually smiled. He said, "That's Alice in Wonderland."

"Jesus," Hull said, getting up. "Good-bye."

● ● ● ● ● ●

"Wheldon here."

"Hull Rainer."

"Ah, Mr Rainer, how do you do. What d'you think of my idea for an appearance on telly?"

"Yes, I'll do it."

"I can give you a minute and half after the ten o'clock news tonight. I'll shave the movie and shave the news."

"What time do you want me there, nine-thirty?"

"Oh, it won't be live, Mr Rainer. We tape everything nowadays. I'm afraid you're a little out of touch."

Hull said coldly, "I am not out of touch, old man. I'm an actor, not a newscaster."

"To be sure, yes. Sorry. Could we possibly have you here about an hour from now?"

After ringing off, Hull dialled another number, one he had memorised. The call signal went unanswered.

Hull stepped out of the street telephone kiosk. He looked at his watch. There was time, he decided. He went to his car.

Ten minutes later, he was at the door of Nan Mountford's flat. He rang, knocked, rang, knocked. The call signal had been right. He returned to the car.

Checking his watch, he thought: Half an hour. He pushed in a cassette, lit a cigarette and sank low in the seat. Neither the music nor the smoke helped. He felt oppressed.

Elsie's behaviour. That, Hull thought, might be a clue. Not, of course, the talk Wilkinson had picked up, theatre gossip swollen by hindsight, so that a sharp exchange becomes a row, a sniffle a flood of tears. But there was a basis in fact. Elsie had been quite different lately. Moody. Silent. Withdrawn. At the time, it hadn't seemed particularly strange.

There was a squeal of brakes. Hull looked up to see a cab stopping outside the block of flats. A girl got out and handed money to the driver.

Hastily, Hull climbed from the car. Throwing his cigarette away, he was about to sprint forward when he realised that although Nan Mountford had seen him, she was making no move to escape. She stood watching him solemnly.

He walked on, producing a reassuring smile. Beside the girl he stopped and said, warmly, "Hello, darling."

"Hello. Seen this?"

She handed him a newspaper. It was an early edition of the evening run. One of the photographs on the front page was of himself, a publicity shot. He looked up.

Nan's expression he now recognised. It was awe. All anyone ever needs, he thought, is to get his picture in the papers. It confers on him instant specialness.

"Poor Elsie," Hull said, giving the paper back. "I'm terribly cut up about all this. No one knows what I'm going through. Even though we're not in love with one another, even though our marriage is only for professional convenience, I'm very fond of her. She's a wonderful person. I'll be shattered if anything's happened to her."

Don't overdo it, he warned himself.

The girl asked, "Professional convenience?"

In a low voice, Hull explained that many show business people married for stability, and to keep off the wolves or sirens, and to help from getting involved in affairs, which were injurious to work.

He ended, "But it's a lonely life at times. When I saw you the other night—well, I don't know, but something happened to me inside. I felt a sort of warmth. You were so beautiful. Your eyes were so *simpatico*."

Watch it, he warned.

"I didn't really think I recognised you," he went on, smiling sadly. "That was a line. But I had to meet you, talk to you. At that moment, you had become something important in my life."

The girl's eyes were shining with moisture, her mouth was slightly open. Whether she was moved by flattery, or was seeing herself as a protagonist in a dramatic, highly publicised mystery, Hull was unable to say. He knew, however, that the spell was to his benefit.

He said, "But as far as anyone else is concerned, the occasion was quite ordinary. We met, we had dinner, we went to your place and talked. We sat and talked until midnight. That's all you need to say, should anyone ask."

He took her hand. "It would be easy enough, wouldn't it?"

Nan Mountford nodded. "Yes."

Hull kissed the hand. "Good-bye for the present, darling," he said soulfully. "We shall meet again when the world is brighter."

He walked away. Halfway to his car, he glanced back. The girl was still standing there. Hull was considerably cheered. He thought: Don't talk to me about acting.

The Wembly studios of UK-TV were in a new high-rise. The pale building rose abruptly from among the semi-detached houses dressed in red brick, a Snow White with seven thousand dwarfs.

The lobby, immense, was deeply carpeted even on the walls. The modern furniture looked to have been designed for contortionists. There were so many reception desks that Hull went out again and asked the doorman.

"I'll telephone from here, sir. What was the name?"

Back in the lobby, Hull, as instructed, sat down to wait. The chair was surprisingly comfortable. Hull relaxed. He was still feeling a small trill of pleasure from the doorman's reaction to his name.

Things were slightly better, Hull thought. A ransom seemed unlikely at this stage, Nan Mountford would probably back up his story, and he was about to get television exposure to several million people.

Hull saw the doorman slip in, whisper briefly to a girl at the nearest desk, slip out again. The girl looked across at Hull, got up and went to the next desk.

Soon it seemed to Hull that everyone in the lobby was casting him surreptitious glances. He didn't mind in the least, but he did wish he had paused outside to straighten himself up a bit.

"Good afternoon, Mr Rainer."

Charles Wheldon was a small man in a black velvet suit and a black sweater with a polo neck. He was bald and in his early forties, which he appeared to be trying to disguise with a boyish grin and a hand that repeatedly covered his pate.

He asked jovially, "Ready for the fray?"

"Sure."

"That's the spirit. Now, I'll tell you what we'll do. First we'll trot along to the bar and have a drink. Your scriptwriter's going to meet us there, and you two can thresh it out between you."

"A script, eh?"

"Yes, much better than off-the-cuffly. Next, we shunt you down to look over a few sets. I'd like you to pick out a corner or a chair or whatever that vaguely resembles something in your house."

"Flat."

"Of course. The old human interest, you know. Best if they think it's from a home, not the studio. Mm?"

"Sure."

"Next," Wheldon said, "we shunt you into Make-up. I'll have a word with your girl myself. Needs a special touch, I think."

Standing back, he looked at Hull with half-closed eyes. He said, "Yes. Heavy on the shadow, a bit of grimness round the mouth, hair a bit looser. Agreed?" He didn't wait for an answer. "Next, two or three rehearsals—they save cutting—and then we shoot. Two hours should see us clear of it all."

"Fine. How about that drink?"

As they moved across the lobby, Wheldon said, "You won't be having a director, so I'll just give you my own thoughts on the motif. I've been thinking motif strongly. Pathos. That's it. Mm?"

"Whatever you say."

"Good. It's lucky you're an actor. You know the bit. The tremor, the hesitation, the slow blink. You'll be fine."

"Yes."

"By the way," Wheldon said, hand to baldness, "sorry about Miss Vanetti. I do hope she's all right."

"Thanks."

Hull spent half an hour with the scriptwriter, five minutes selecting a desk and a stretch of blank wall, and fifteen minutes being made up—memorising his lines at the same time. He was taken back to the set.

The desk was the centre of blazing lights. Half a dozen men moved about. It was, "Over here, Mr Rainer." "Thank you, Mr Rainer." "Ready, Mr Rainer?"

This can't be bad, Hull thought. This can't be bad at all.

7

"The scarf, green, is by Jaqumar," the television news reader said. "The fawn raincoat is London Fog, made in the United States, oddly enough. Her shoes are by Vernon Humpage of Blackpool. Underclothing is St Michael. Her dress, pale grey, has no label and was bought off the peg in Portobello Road."

Jason and Jenny were intent on their rented TV. Jason's attention was physical. Knowing the facts being given, he had stopped listening. He was dwelling with pleasure on the news of the latest theory which was being put forward.

Although not discounting murder, kidnapping, suicide, death by misadventure, elopement, or voluntary seclusion, the police were considering strongly the possibility of a political abduction. Many radical groups could be responsible, from IRA offshoots to Arab terrorists. The motive would be an exchange: Elsie Vanetti for prisoners in British gaols. A likely contender was the Scottish Freedom Action League, a member of which was at present on hunger strike in prison.

Jason's pleasure was not mere amusement. All these international angles could do nothing but good for his cause.

Before the discussion of theory on the newscast, there had been film clips. The first showed a crowd milling outside a City cafeteria; a table inside; detectives talking to a Negress and a middle-aged woman, the latter pair staring as if terrified at the camera. The second was a brief interview with a Bill Finegan, stage-door keeper, the last person to have seen Elsie Vanetti. The third film clip showed Chief Inspector Harold Wilkinson walking through a group of pressmen and shaking his head.

Jason became alert when he heard from the TV commentator:

"Getting back to the purse found today. It is understood the police are puzzled as to its appearance in the cafe, since no one even distantly resembling Miss Vanetti was noticed there. It would seem to rule out a criminal kidnapping—the gang would use the identification to prove they held Miss Vanetti captive. It leaves other theories open, however.

"Which brings us up to the minute on the Vanetti case. As we've already mentioned, immediately following this newscast we will present an appeal by Miss Vanetti's husband, the well-known actor Hull Rainer. Now to the international scene. In Paris today . . ."

Jason said, "What? What was that?"

Jenny looked around. "Mm?"

"Hull Rainer. He's going to be on in a minute."

"They said so earlier. It must've been before you came. Does it matter?"

"Interesting," Jason said. He rose from the table. "Very interesting."

"Yes, I suppose it will be."

"No, I mean as an experiment. With Elsie."

"I get you," Jenny said. She lowered the volume on the TV. "Let Elsie watch her husband."

"Right. It'll be a marvellous test. Could be dangerous, too. I don't know if I've got him completely out of her memory yet. Visually perhaps. But incidents, no, there're dozens and dozens she still retains."

"She won't see anything like that."

"Still. An article of clothing could do the trick. Remember, I told you how one item might trigger a sort of chain reaction until the subject recalls the whole person."

"Here it wouldn't matter, dear."

"But it might undo what I've already done."

"So leave it."

Jason scrubbed knuckles against the side of his face. "It's such a great opportunity, though."

"You're arguing with yourself," Jenny said, smiling. "Whose side are you on most?"

Jason said, deciding quickly, "The experiment's." He went over to the bedroom door. "Back in a minute."

Elsie was curled up on the bed, asleep. Her hands were clasped under her chin. Her face was sweetly in repose. Untidy hair and grimy raincoat ignored, she looked like an advertisement for a bedtime drink.

Jason, by the door, gazed at her for a moment, his head moving to a sideways tilt. As always when here in this room, which was commonplace and close to sordid, he had a feeling of peace.

He went softly to the bed. Bending over, he brushed a hank of hair from the girl's brow, then with his fingertips gently stroked her cheek. He smiled.

Jason straightened his face abruptly, thinking: Is this the way to wake someone up? She isn't a sick child. She's a grown woman.

He put a heavy hand on her shoulder.

When presently Jason brought Elsie onto the landing, she was in her customary waking state—a light trance. Jason placed her in a chair facing the television set.

On the screen, men in track suits were running across a field.

Jason said, "Elsie, I want you to watch carefully. You will see different people. One of them may be known to you. If so, please tell me. You understand?"

"Yes," the actress said quietly. Her eyes, lazy, were fixed on the screen.

Jason moved to stand where he could watch the TV from the side of his vision while having a three-quarter profile view of Elsie's face.

The screen had been taken over by the weather man. Jenny turned up the volume and went back to her seat. She glanced at Elsie: an expression combining compassion and apology.

The weather man talked on, slashing with crayon at charts. His speech was clipped and rapid, as if he worked in dread of being understood.

Jason waited. He was growing impatient. His hands, he realised, were clenched. He relaxed them and told himself it was going to be all right.

The commentator came back. He said expansively, "And that brings us to the end of "Scene Tonight," your ten o'clock news coverage from here and abroad. After a short break for sponsor time, we'll be taking you into the home of Hull Rainer, the husband of Elsie Vanetti. Good night."

Jason snapped his full attention to the actress. She had stiffened. Her eyes were unwavering on the screen, which was alive with flashing commercials, yet her hovering frown seemed to be for something else.

Jason nodded. He understood. It was the name. Not her husband's —her own. It was one of the details he had planned on leaving for obliteration until the very last. There would be no point in calling her Elsie if she didn't know that was her name.

The last commercial flashed off. The screen was blank for a moment. Next, the camera was trucking in on a man at a desk. He leaned forward. He gave a faint, sad smile as the camera came to a stop.

Jason watched Elsie. He was unaware of his clenched fists. The actress was still frowning.

"Elsie, darling," Hull Rainer said in a low voice. "I want you to know that I am here waiting for you. I want to see you again. I want to hear you, even if it's only on the telephone. Elsie, please don't delay in . . ."

Rainer talked on.

The actress was watching him intently. Her frown was deeper. She sat in a forward lean. There appeared in her attitude some manner of recognition.

Could be the voice, Jason told himself nervously. Must be. That and the repeated name. So good. Great. Couldn't be better. The voice could be erased from her mind after showing, whereas if this hadn't come on she might have been triggered by it later.

Rainer had switched to addressing a person or persons unknown, asking that he be informed by anyone who knew the whereabouts of his wife. He appealed to those who might be close to her to contact him as soon as possible, to please not delay any longer.

"I'm waiting here," Hull Rainer ended, looking down. "I'm waiting."

A pause, and the screen faded to blank.

Jenny got up. She switched off the TV with a vicious swipe of her hand. "Christ," she said.

Jason saw there were tears in her eyes. He told her, "Steady, Jen."

Jenny blinked and smiled. "The poor bastard. Did you see the way his hand trembled?"

"Jen."

"What are we *doing* to these people?"

"Darling, don't upset yourself."

Jenny sagged. She sighed and said, "I'm tired, Jason. I think I'll go to bed."

"All right."

Turning away, she went into the front bedroom. Jason looked at Elsie. Her face was free from lines, bland as a manikin. She had leaned back in the chair.

Jason asked, "Did you see anyone you knew?"

"I—I don't think so."

"A voice. Did you recognise a voice?"

"Yes," Elsie said at once.

"Who does it belong to?"

"I'm not sure."

Jason was satisfied, even quietly elated. He said, "Listen to me, Elsie."

● ● ● ● ● ●

The following morning, Jason again went out for the papers and to eat breakfast. Not wishing to make his face too familiar, he chose a different cafe. It was a snack bar without tables. He sat on a stool at the counter, ordered pancakes and read his newspapers.

The story was still number one. As often mentioned as Elsie was her husband. The text of his appeal was given verbatim. There were editorials on his earnestness and strength. He was there in photographs, press and posed.

Other pictures showed the recovered purse, the Equity card, a Black woman pointing dramatically at a table, Chief Inspector Wilkinson talking with a girl who claimed to have found the purse first.

The *Telegraph* offered an exclusive interview with an authority on terrorist groups. The *Express* had an exclusive interview with the actress' mother, Mrs Maud Vanetti. The *Mirror* had an exclusive interview with the cashier of the cafe.

In respect of the investigation, Interpol was involved, midnight raids had been made by the Special Branch on houses in Belfast, Glasgow and Cardiff, three figures of London's underworld had been detained for questioning, and police in New York were looking for a man who, when Elsie Vanetti was appearing on Broadway, had sent her a threatening letter.

Jason enjoyed his meal and his read. He went home and set confidently to work with the actress.

After telling her she was in no physical discomfort (the bath complaints of Jenny in mind), Jason sent Elsie straight through from a light trance to a profound without pausing at the medium stage. The process took a satisfying two and a quarter minutes. Jason reckoned to have it down soon to one minute or less.

He decided, however, to test.

Taking the pin from his waistband, he said, "Hold out your right hand, please."

Elsie's hand came up obediently. Jason took it, isolated a finger and closed in with the pin.

And stopped. He couldn't seem to bring himself to plunge the point into the finger. Licking his lips, he tried again. No good. His hand, as before, began its lunge and then drew back. His arm began to ache.

Ridiculous, Jason thought, sweating slightly. I've done this at least a thousand times. I've done it to myself. I've done it to Jenny.

He tried again. The result was the same.

He told himself that the act was, after all, rather brutal, more so as his subject had not come to him of her own accord. It was that mainly, the latter, which he felt was holding him back.

Tossing the pin aside, he turned to another test.

"Elsie," he said, "there is someone knocking on the ceiling. Hear it?"

She shook her head slowly.

"Yes you can. Listen very hard. There, you can hear it now. Please count the knocks. Listen and count."

Elsie, giving small nods, said, "One . . . two . . . three . . ."

"Good," Jason cut in. "It's stopped now."

He went and sprawled comfortably on the bed. The session began.

It went smoothly. Jason took Elsie backwards and forwards in time, reminding, asking, cancelling. Often, when Elsie's pleasure was apparent, he would dwell overlong on a particular event or person, this because he delighted in seeing her smile as she brought out details. Unconsciously, he smiled with her.

It saddened him a little that on these occasions he was forced to say, "Forget that. Erase it from your mind." It was like taking back a gift. But he reminded himself that in a few weeks Elsie would own her memory treasures again.

Towards the morning's end, the talk was in a different mood. Elsie, frowning, was telling about a boating trip with schoolfriends which had turned out badly, near tragically. A storm had come up, the boat had capsized, one of the girls had come close to drowning.

Subject exhausted, Jason asked the customary, "Does it remind you of anything that happened later?"

"Happened? No."

"Does it remind you of anything at all?"

She seemed to be pondering. At length she said, "Yes, that black cloud."

"What does it remind you of?"
Elsie said, "Something evil."

● ● ● ● ● ●

Jason sat at the table, moodily eating a sandwich. He made no answer when Jenny called, from the kitchen, "She seemed to like the cold cuts."

Jason was thinking that he would have to go over the play again with Elsie. He had believed he had eradicated it from her memory. This, patently, was not so. The other actors and the plot were gone, but she still retained the essence of the play, its driving force. He may have to go so far as to get hold of the script and read it aloud to her to . . .

A pounding sounded on the front door below.

Jason's body jerked. The sandwich flipped from his hand.

Jenny quickly came in to the doorway of the kitchen. Her face was tensely open in a grin. She said, "My God, what's that?"

"Quiet," Jason hissed. "Listen." He was frightened.

The pounding came again.

Jenny said, whispering, "It can't be anyone we know. We told everybody we'd be away this month."

"Salesman," Jason snapped. "Could be anything. Postman with a parcel."

"We're not expecting one."

He hated her.

She said, "We won't answer. Let them knock."

"Yes."

"We'll just wait till they go away."

He liked her again. But it was no good. "If it's someone we know, someone we didn't tell, they might think something's happened to us. They could break in."

"Or they could get the police to break in," Jenny said. She was holding on to the doorframe with both hands. "Jesus."

Jason got up swiftly. He crossed to the front bedroom, went inside and over to the bay window. With caution he peered down through the lace curtains.

He could see nothing by the front door because of the portico, its top littered with rusting beer cans and cigarette packets gone white in the elements.

Jenny's whisper came through to him: "I think they've given up."

Cruelly, the pounding sounded again, lasting longer than before.

Jason looked at the street. There was no vehicle that resembled a police car. He knew, in fact, every car present.

Going back to the landing, he said, "Telegram. Drains inspection. Someone looking for a former tenant." He was actually talking to himself.

"We'll have to answer?" Jenny asked.

Jason moved to the head of the stairs. Starting down, he said, "I think it's best. They'd only come back. Let's get it done with."

Jenny came to the bannister and leaned over. She whispered, "I'm scared, Jason."

"Don't be silly," he snapped. He allowed himself to feel angry. It helped.

That pounding came again. The cause was either a shoe or a weighty fist. The door dithered.

Jason was midway down. He kept on going despite the hiss from behind of, "Don't do it. Let's wait."

His pulses were sending out taps of pain like Morse code. He told himself he was a fool, and he told himself he was doing the right thing.

Moving off the bottom step, indecision hurried his nerves to such an extent that he strode quickly to the door. He gasped, drew it open.

He drew the door a foot from the jamb. His condition paused in its deterioration when he saw through the space the massive form of Mrs Ratch.

She was the landlord's wife. An Irishwoman nearly six feet tall, she weighed in excess of two hundred and fifty pounds, the bulk exaggerated by a flowing raglan coat of thick tweed.

"Took you long enough," she said.

Jason stated, "I was having a nap." He tried to hold his features steady.

"Odd time of day for that."

He shrugged.

Mrs Ratch had a broad, plain face. It was so covered with freckles that from a distance it looked to be tanned. A turban-tied scarf hid her hair. She had small, sharp eyes.

Mrs Ratch often wore a vacant smile. It had no meaning. She was not smiling at the moment.

Neither was Jason. His nervousness had paused only, not begun to fade. And now the pause ended.

Mrs Ratch put an oversize hand on the door, pushed it open and stepped inside. She did so while clicking on and off a smile and saying:

"Won't bother you long, Mr Galt."

"Listen," Jason stammered.

The woman was already at the foot of the stairs. She moved agilely on legs which shrunk from gross calves to surprisingly petite ankles.

Jason managed, "I'm busy."

Mrs Ratch started up. "Won't detain you, Mr Galt. Nice spot of weather we're having, eh?"

Jason was torn between restraining the visitor and guarding the open door. If he closed it he felt he would be closing the visitor in.

She had gone a third of the way up.

Jason slammed the door shut. He strode to the staircase and took the first three steps as one. Drawing level with Mrs Ratch, he grasped her arm.

"Now, just a minute," he said fiercely.

She stopped. She looked at him. Her face was taut with imperiousness, like a challenged teacher who knows she's wrong.

"Yes, Mr Galt?"

"Just you hold on a minute."

Heavily polite: "*Yes*, Mr Galt?"

"You can't come barging in here this way."

"Barging," the woman repeated, as if trying to recall the definition. She looked away and up. "Hello there."

"Hello," Jenny said bleakly.

Jason was telling himself urgently to get cool. At once. It was insane to antagonise the woman. She could cause endless problems. She could, out of spite, send a whole stream of callers, the old harassment routine.

"Nice spot of weather," Mrs Ratch said.

Jenny nodded. "Lovely." She wore a harsh grin.

Dropping his restraining hand, Jason said in a pleasant tone, "We've paid the rent. Didn't your husband tell you?"

"Yes, Mr Galt."

"We always have."

"I know," Mrs Ratch said. "You're prompt, I'll say that for you." She moved on up the stairs. "No, it's not the rent."

"Oh?"

"It's the electric meter."

Jason remembered. It was a factor he should have reckoned on. The coin-in-the-slot meter was emptied every six weeks—by Ratch, his wife or their agent.

Next, Jason remembered that the meter was in Elsie's room. He was taken by a shiver.

Mrs Ratch reached the head of the stairs. In a pitying voice she asked, "How are you, dear?"

Jenny said, "Fine." She backed away.

Mrs Ratch smiled at her while looking skippingly around the landing. Her smile faded.

"What's all this, then?" she asked.

Jason stopped at her side. He was breathless, as if he had climbed a thousand steps. "What's what?"

"All this. The furniture."

Jason and Jenny looked at each other helplessly. Jason was worrying about the meter. He was unable to switch to the landing.

Jenny said, "Damp."

"The front room can't be damp."

"It is."

That imperious look came back. "In this weather? Really now."

"It's only a little, Mrs Ratch."

Jason's wandering gaze rested on the shoes poking out from under the couch. He interrupted his main worry to insist to himself: They're just shoes like a million others.

"Oh, well," the woman said. "And anyway, it looks all right here. So roomy, these landings. Such fine property."

Jenny, back in her place by the kitchen doorway, said in a jerky stream, "Yes, it is. It's fine property. I've often said that. It's a shame these houses have to go. I call it a disgrace. It's a . . . a disgrace." She came to a drab halt.

"Thank you. I agree. Lot of bloody Communists, this council."

"Yes."

Mrs Ratch squared her vast shoulders. "Still, I mustn't stay nattering. Got to get on."

She moved, heading for the back room.

Jason went forward in long strides. He passed Mrs Ratch and swung around with his back to the door. The woman came to a swaying halt. She said a bewildered, "Eh?"

"You can't go in there," Jason said, breathless again.

Mrs Ratch stared. The bewilderment went. She made her face hideous with a sneer. It caused Jason to blink in confusion and panic.

"I see," the woman said. "That's it."

"What?"

"You're like all the others."

"What?"

"Oh, don't think I don't know the angles," Mrs Ratch said, menacing her freckled face forward, at the same time making a belligerent grab for her hips. "You're leaving soon, so you thought you could get away with it."

"I don't understand."

"Foreign coins? Old fashioned ha'pennies? Washers exactly the right size that you can buy five hundred for a quid? Plastic discs? Don't stand there and tell me you don't understand."

"Yes, I do now."

"I've been in this game a long time, sonny."

Jason aimed for, and achieved, a smile. He said, "Mrs Ratch, you've got the wrong impression. There's nothing in your electric meter but good English money. As you'll see for yourself."

The sneer weakened. "You stopped me."

"Mrs Ratch, there's someone in bed in here. A couple."

As if absently, the woman said, "By the terms of the contract, subletting or renting of rooms is strictly—"

"They're here for two days."

"Oh."

"Friends," Jason said. "From Dublin."

Mrs Ratch grunted. It appeared to signify an apology. Which she appeared to abnegate with, "Late to be in bed."

Jenny offered, "Party last night."

The woman looked at her, then at Jason, then back again at Jenny. She asked, "Is there something wrong with you two?"

"Very much so," Jason said. "We're hung-over."

Jenny added, "And you caught us in the middle of an argument."

Mrs Ratch smiled. "Well, there you are."

From beyond the door at his back, Jason heard a shuffling sound. He thought, with a strange and frightening calm: Elsie is going to knock on the door.

He said, "If you can come back another time, Mrs Ratch."

"What, three miles?"

"In fifteen minutes, then. Meanwhile we'll rouse our friends."

The woman mused aloud, "I do have the next-door meter to empty."

"Fine."

"But it's not good for me, you know. Up and down these stairs. Why don't I just slip in the room quietly? I won't bother your friends."

The shuffling sound was drawing closer to the door.

Jenny said, "They're honeymooners."

Mrs Ratch tutted. She swung around, saying, "All right, then, I'll go and do the other meter."

"Thank you."

The woman still hadn't moved, apart from the turn. She looked at the bathroom. She asked, "D'you think I could—you know?"

"Of course," Jason said quickly. "Help yourself."

Mrs Ratch smiled. "Excuse me," she said in a delicate voice.

The shuffling sound was right behind the door. It ended there.

Mrs Ratch moved forward. And a knock sounded.

Jenny made a small whimper-like cry. Jason whirled with his fist raised. Mrs Ratch glanced back.

She saw her tenant knock on the door, heard him ask, "Are you awake in there?" She went on and to the bathroom and closed herself in.

Jason gasped, breathless again. His weakness of relief lasted mere seconds. He twisted the handle, pushed the door. It stopped a few inches from the jamb.

"Move back," he hissed. "Step away, Elsie."

The door eased open. After shooting Jenny an urgent look, Jason slipped into the room.

Elsie was standing there. She said, "Bathroom."

"Yes. In a minute. Come with me."

He took her arm, led her out and along the landing. He fretted at her slowness.

Jenny whispered, "Why don't you wait till she's gone?"

"Don't want her back. Let's get rid of her."

He took Elsie into the front room. "Wait here," he said. He came out and closed the door.

A sound of water flushing.

Jason gestured to Jenny. Together they went quickly and noisily down the stairs. Jason opened the front door, calling, "Good-bye for now! See you soon!" Jenny echoed his words. Jason slammed the door.

They went to the foot of the stairs and started up. Jenny took Jason's arm. He could feel the tremble in her hand.

Mrs Ratch appeared at the stairhead. "That was quick."

"They're as nervous as cats," Jason said, succeeding with another smile.

The woman returned it while looking across the landing. She said, "That damp in the front room."

Jason and Jenny came level with her. Jason said brusquely, "It's nothing. Forget it. We like the furniture out here."

"Such large landings."

He pointed toward the open rear door. "The meter's all yours, Mrs Ratch."

● ● ● ● ● ●

Later that day, Jason was returning home from a walk in the nearby park. Darkness had fallen. The air was crisp, as refreshing as a breeze at tropic noon.

Jason felt fine. In respect of the landlord's wife, the ugly incident was over. Mrs Ratch's final comment of possible danger—"The bedroom looks different"—had been soothed by Jenny saying, "We traded the furniture and made a profit."

A future danger, that of the woman connecting the reappeared actress, the unseen couple in the back room, and himself, Jason had concluded was a misty possibility which he must live with and pray against.

He was not perturbed. The incident loomed in his mind greater for his own behaviour than the danger. He was distressed by his weaknesses, yet proud of his moments of strength and decision. Several times he had been surprised by his presence of mind, especially when he had repeated Elsie's knock to give the impression that hers had been his.

On the whole, he thought he had come through Mrs Ratch's visit with a plus. It was a good sign.

Jason turned into Shank Place and strode along to Number Nine. He was looking forward to another two or three hours' work with Elsie.

Jason had closed the door behind him before seeing Jenny. She was sitting on the stairs, sitting on the bottom step smiling at him brightly. It seemed a real smile.

He said, amused-puzzled, "Hello."

"Hi."

"What's up with you? Looking forward to your walk?"

"Walk," she said with a snort.

He laughed. "Jen, I don't get it."

"It's gorgeous," she said, squeezing her shoulders in. "I can't wait to tell you. Yes, I can. It's a fab wait."

"I'll kick you."

Jenny bounced up, came to him and clasped his arms. Her face became happily solemn, her eyes carrying on the mouth's smile. She said:

"Good news, Jason."

"Tell me."

"It was on the radio just after you left. In a newscast."

"Tell me."

"A reward's been posted."

"Oh?"

"By the UK chapter of the Vanetti fan club. Guess how much."

"I can't."

She pressed his arms tightly. "Twenty-five thousand pounds."

It was Jason's turn to snort. "Impossible. A fan club?"

"Darling, you don't understand. These fan clubs. Some of them have half a million members. If Elsie's only has fifty thousand, it's enough. They chip in an old ten-bob note apiece. It's nothing."

"Twenty-five thousand pounds," Jason said, believing.

"For information leading to the safe return of Miss Elsie Vanetti."

"My God."

"That's what I said myself."

"Twenty-five thousand."

"It's a fortune."

"Right."

"We'll be rich," Jenny said, clapping her hands, her smile coming back. She moved away, walking in a circle. She held her hands up in the clap position while talking.

"I've thought it all out. I've been sitting here planning. I think I've got it perfect. Tell me how it sounds. We take Elsie, dear valuable Elsie, to an empty house that's for sale. Oh, I forgot to mention, we pick out the house first, it must have a garden, and go to the agent to ask the price and so on."

Jason said, "Jen."

"That's so he'll back up our story, our reason for being there. Anyway, we take Elsie to the garden, put her in a shed or something, then I hurry to telephone the police and say we've found someone who looks like the missing actress."

"Jen."

"Beforehand, you'll have given her back her memory. All of it except for the past few days. There'll be no risk. Oh, and we'll go to several agents enquiring about houses. The more the merrier."

Jason said a firm, "Jenny."

Jenny stopped walking. She was faced the other way. She dropped her arms slowly and slowly turned. Her body had lost its vibrancy. Jason realised that the glee, now gone, had been mainly artificial, an act.

She said, making a statement, "You won't do it."

He shook his head in confirmation.

"I knew all along," she said. "I was kidding myself."

"I can't, Jen."

"Can't bear to let her go?"

"What?"

She came to him swiftly and grasped the reverse of his windcheater. "Twenty-five thousand pounds, darling. Wealth. You only need to give me five. You'll be rich. Without danger. Rich and free. You could produce your own show. Your name would have got known for finding Elsie."

"No, Jen."

"There'd be no more of this. No more things like Mrs rotten Ratch. It's wearing me out, being here day after day. You've got work to do. I've got nothing to do but worry. It could easily go wrong. I don't want to go to prison. I've had enough of dreariness."

"I'm sorry."

Jenny subsided. Her hands fell. She said quietly, "Jason."

"Yes?"

"Think it over. Please. I'll go out for my walk. You weigh it up carefully. Money and no risk now, against a doubtful future. Will you do that? Will you?"

He nodded.

Jenny stepped back. There was little hope in her mien. She gave him a tired smile, went to the door, left the house.

Jason went upstairs. He lowered himself onto the couch with a sigh and sat, leaning forward. Absently, he reached underneath and brought out the brick and a shoe. This had become a habit. But now he made no attempt to work at wearing the sole. He ran his fingers over the shoe's uppers thoughtfully.

Jason's cogitation was short. Although impressed by the size of the reward, he felt no temptation. Only one half of his aim would be satisfied. Jenny's idea of him producing his own show was naive, as was her thinking that the mere finding of Elsie would grant him celebrity. So, no reward. Jason told himself he had his ego to consider.

He sat on, quite comfortable, his fingers caressing the shoe.

8

The day after Hull Rainer appeared on television, his telephone hardly went for more than five minutes without ringing. He heard from people whose existence he had almost forgotten. Strangers rang up to say they wished him luck. Other strangers, voices muffled, asked where he had hidden his wife's body. A water diviner offered his assistance. A BBC-TV producer, with whom Hull had worked before, said, more in sorrow than anger, that Hull should have gone to him for his television appearance. The male owner of a youthful voice said he and Elsie Vanetti were living together in the South of France.

To escape the telephone, Hull went downstairs and talked to the reporters. They took his picture, he answered questions, he made a solemn statement. He was impressed to learn that two of the men were from foreign newspapers, Chicago and Rome.

The telephone was ringing in wait when he went back. It continued like that until eleven at night, at which point he took the receiver off its cradle and went to bed. He slept well.

In the morning, he dressed with his usual care and hummed as he fixed breakfast. Eating, he read the papers—read, that is, the parts relating to himself. The pictures had come out well and the copy was favourable.

As for the rest of the Vanetti Affair, which Hull skimmed over, nothing had changed. The purse was still a mystery. There were no claimants for the reward. New York's author of the threatening letter had been found, in prison; he was a burglar whose side-line was writing letters of menace to newsmakers. Elsie Vanetti was reported to have been seen in a dozen parts of Britain and in twenty foreign countries. A man in Melbourne had confessed to her murder. In London, the detained underworld figures had been released.

After breakfast, realising the telephone's silence, Hull remembered it was still disconnected. He righted that. The first call came three minutes later. So it went, a repeat of yesterday at a less frantic pace, until close to noon.

"This is Arthur Jarrold of the *Sunday Standard*."

"No development," Hull said automatically. "No fresh statement."

"Wait, Mr Rainer. This is not the news department. I'm the features editor. I have a commercial proposition for you."

"Such as?"

In a persuasive tone the man went on, "We thought we'd try to do a two-part on your wife, Mr Rainer, on her as seen by you. A first-person thing. 'My Life With Elsie.' That stuff. Does it sound interesting?"

"I simply don't have the time to write it, Mr Jarrold."

"Oh, we wouldn't want you to do the writing yourself. It would have to be in *Standard* style. We'd put a ghost on it."

"I see."

"Interested?"

"That depends on how much you'd pay."

"Seven thousand."

Hull blinked. His cheek twitched. "Seven thousand pounds?"

"Yes, Mr Rainer. There would, of course, be clauses pertaining to your wife's reappearance, and we'd like to sign you exclusively for the aftermath stuff."

"That sounds all right," Hull murmured. He was stunned.

"Could you come in today? The sooner we get this show on the road the better. Four this afternoon would be good. We'll have the contracts ready by then and you can chat to the ghost. A couple of hours, that's all she'll need. Four o'clock?"

"Yes, fine," Hull said, ruffling himself alert. "And the money?"

"We'll give you a check on signature of contract. I take it we have a deal."

"We have."

"Great, Mr Rainer. See you later."

Hull put the receiver down slowly. Turning away, he began to circle the four couches. He shook his head in wonderment, thinking of the seven thousand pounds. He couldn't believe it was that simple.

The doorchimes sounded. Hull went to the door and drew it open. Standing there was a young constable with a package. He handed it over, saying, "Miss Vanetti's purse, sir, with Inspector Wilkinson's compliments."

"Did he find any prints?"

"No, sir."

The telephone rang as Hull returned to the living room. He went across, lifted the hand-set, chanted his number.

"Hi, baby. George here. What's new?"

"Nothing," Hull said. The disgruntled thought came to him that George Case, his agent, may have set up the *Sunday Standard* deal, therefore be in for a bite of the takings.

"Listen. This is hot. Can you get down here right away?"

"What cooks?"

"Explain later. I'm in the Royal Arms. Get down here soonest. You're hot."

"I'm on my way," Hull said, mystified but expectant, and pleased that George hadn't mentioned the *Sunday Standard*.

He left the flat and went down to the lobby. His car he would leave; parking was too difficult in the West End.

Only two reporters were standing outside. They broke from their casual stances at Hull's appearance and asked, simultaneously, "Any news?"

"No. I think it's too late for that. She would have called me by now, and kidnappers would have made contact."

One man grinned. "Maybe they have but you're not saying."

Hull shrugged. "Where is everybody?"

"Followed the cops to Wapping. A lighterman pulled a woman's body from the river this morning."

Hull felt queasy. "Dead?"

"Sure."

"Could it be—er—?"

The reporter said, "*I* don't think so."

Reprieved, Hull nodded. "Neither do I. My wife is an excellent swimmer."

The other man said, "But even swimmers can drown—if they want to."

Hull snapped, "Thanks and good-bye."

He found a taxi at the end of the road. During the drive to Wardour Street, London's motion-picture centre, he decided to make no mention of the *Sunday Standard* to George Case. The wily agent might find some way of squirming in on the deal.

The Royal Arms pub was packed with noontime drinkers. All were connected with the outer fringes of the movie business. The higher lamas drank elsewhere.

Hull knew every face. He knew every crack and picture on the walls. It was the same with other places in the locale. Hull seemed to have spent half his life waiting around Wardour Street.

George Case stood at the bar. He was medium height, plump, fifty years old. A heavy, thick-featured face was topped by hair in the style of Rudolph Valentino. He wore a tan suit and a rainbow tie. All his mannerisms derived from those of agents in movies about Hollywood. His accent was mid-Atlantic.

"Baby," he said, putting an arm around Hull. "I caught your show on little brother the other night. You were great, but great."

"Thanks."

"And now you're hot."

"You've got me something, George?"

"There're one or two things in the air. I'm talking to people. But there could be something on the front burner right now, five minutes from here."

"Stop playing for suspense, George."

"Remember a thing called *The Road Turns Back?*"

It was a best-selling novel of last year. "Sure," Hull said. "I read it. Everybody and his dog read it."

"So Finegold bought the rights. He's casting. There's a part he hasn't filled yet. The kid. Remember?"

Hull did. The part would be third male lead, an immense jump for an actor of Hull's rating.

Excited, he asked, "Is it possible? You've asked him?"

"Slow down, baby," George Case said. "We'll do this *my* way. We don't ask, we *get* asked. If we're lucky. And we should be. You're hot. Let's go."

They went out and along the street. George said, "Sammy Finegold's shrewd—todaywise. He won't stop to think the Vanetti thing'll be forgotten a few months from now."

Coolly, Hull said, "I can act as well, you know."

"You're only the best, baby, that's all. Would I handle a bum?"

The restaurant was the latest "in" place for showpeople, those who could afford its prices. It had a bar in the foyer and then steps leading down to a mirror-walled room packed with small tables.

Hull and George went down the steps. They stopped to look around. The buzz of conversation lessened in volume as, first, people glanced their way, then stared. Hull was the centre of attraction. He felt marvellous.

The headwaiter came. George told him, "We're looking for someone, Antonio. Don't bother about us." He moved off. Hull followed. He allowed a mist of suffering to come into his eyes.

By a table where sat a swarthy man and a girl who looked sixteen, George came to a stop that had the unbalance of the unplanned. His face bore an expression of pleased surprise.

"Why, hello there, Mr Finegold," he said, reaching out a hand.

The man rose. While letting his hand be shaken by the agent, he looked at Hull. He asked, "Mr Rainer, isn't it?"

"Yes, Mr Finegold. How do you do."

"Hello." They shook hands. "Any news of your wife?"

"I'm afraid not."

"Won't you join us, have a glass of wine?"

"Thank you," George said.

Five minutes later, the producer asked Hull, "Ever hear of a book called *The Road Turns Back*?"

● ● ● ● ● ●

At four o'clock, after a late lunch with George Case, Hull was strolling lazily along Fleet Street. He felt in great form. With Samuel Finegold he had talked for an hour about the scheduled movie. Although nothing definite had been decided, the producer was going to mail him a copy of the screenplay. It was an excellent sign.

Hull turned into the *Sunday Standard* building. A clerk took him to the office of Arthur Jarrold. The features editor was a short, fussy man who smelt of liniment. He and Hull and the paper's lawyer went over the contract together. It seemed in order. Hull signed. He was given a check for seven thousand pounds. Still not quite believing, he put the frail-looking piece of paper carefully in his wallet.

The ghost writer turned out to be an outstandingly pretty girl in her mid-twenties who, Jarrold assured Hull before leaving them alone together, was a marvel at the game.

She was a marvel in other ways too, Hull thought. Legs, hips, breasts. A very ripe marvel. While the girl asked questions and made note of answers, Hull enjoyed himself by mentally taking her clothes off. He was sensually stimulated. Had the situation been other than it was, he would have worked hard at dating the girl.

At last they were finished. Out on the street, Hull stopped to look at his check before moving away. He thought about the ghost writer's legs.

LATEST IN VANETTI CASE blared a newsvendor's poster. Hull hurried to him and bought an evening paper. The latest was a negative. The body of a drowned woman, one whom the police thought might have been the actress, had been identified as a German tourist.

Hull put the paper in a rubbish bin and went back to thinking about his ghost's legs.

Impulsively, passing a row of telephone booths, he strode to one that was empty and went inside. His hunger was strong, now that he had been reminded of its existence. He dialled Nan Mountford's number.

"Yes, hello?"

"Nan—Hull Rainer."

"Oh, hello there." Her voice was warm, responsive. "I've been wondering when I'd hear from you again."

"I've been busy every waking moment."

"Poor Hull."

"Darling," he said. "About me being at your place that night. I haven't told the police yet. I've been trying to protect you. But they're getting to be a nuisance about it."

"Tell them, Hull. Do tell them. And how terribly sweet of you, protecting me."

"It's a sordid, dangerous business," Hull said, his tone implying that it was also romantic and exciting. "You'd be better out of it altogether."

"But if the police insist."

"Yes, that's it. So we'd better get our story straight, agree on exactly what we talked of and so on."

"Quite."

"Could I come round there now? I've been cooped up in the flat here for days."

"Come at once, Hull. It'll be lovely to see you."

He took a cab. Sitting back with a cigarette, he told himself this was stupid. If it should get out that, far from waiting unhappily at home for news of his wife, he was dallying with a girl, he would be pilloried in every quarter.

The warning was sensible, Hull knew. Yet it served him only as a stimulant. The piquancy of the venture was heightened by risk.

He paid off the cab and went up to Nan's flat. The door was open. Nan called, "Come in." He went into the living room, where the girl rose from a chair to greet him. She wore a simple skirt-sweater outfit.

Hull took her in his arms. Her body was soft, yielding. He closed his eyes in comfort.

"I'm so glad you came," she whispered.

He kissed her neck, her cheek, her mouth. He roved his tongue inside. He put a hand underneath the sweater.

Nan eased her mouth away to murmur, "Undress me."

Afterwards, they showered together, laughing like children. Hull wearing a towel and Nan a robe, they went into the kitchen to scrounge up a meal. They had corn flakes, scrambled eggs and white wine.

While eating, they went over the alibi. About this, Nan was the serious one. Hull acted. He had lost his worry over Wilkinson's suspicion.

After brandy and a cigarette, they went to bed.

Nan fell asleep. Hull got up and went into the living room for a brandy and a smoke. He felt pleasant, happy with work prospects and the check in his pocket. He told himself smugly that he would not have exchanged places with anyone.

Back in the bedroom, he sat on a stool and looked at the sleeping girl. He looked, and his smile faded. A shudder ran over his body, leaving behind a coldness at the back of his neck.

It had come to him again, that strange desire. He was both frightened and intrigued, as always. The latter emotion usually won. Countless times he had given in to the desire in the afterglow of sex with a semi-stranger. It never came at any other time.

He longed now to awaken the girl and call her a slut. He wanted to revile her as cheap, a tart, a tramp, a piece of dirt. He wanted to see her cringe and cry.

Hull was taken by another shudder. It was more violent than the first. His every part was affected, and drops of brandy leapt from the glass.

Drooping, he stared at Nan Mountford while remembering other girls.

There had been so many. And so few had stood up for themselves. Fear had held their tongues. An unnecessary fear. When on occasion he had resorted to the physical, his slaps across the face had been light, disdainful.

Dwelling on abuse, Hull became more intrigued, less frightened. Realising this moved him to fast, worried action. He jumped up, went back to the other room and started to dress.

The last girl, he reminded himself, with her the slaps had not been as light as he had imagined. She had threatened to go to the police. It had taken an hour of apologetic, persuasive talk and an excuse of drunkenness before she had agreed to drop the matter—so long as she never saw him again.

She never did. Hull never saw any of his girls after the session of abuse. There were plenty more in the city. All with smooth bodies, and all so very young.

Dressed, Hull wrote a note and left the flat. As he walked through the dark, quiet streets, his worry drained. He combed his hair, lit a cigarette, smiled.

9

One week after the disappearance of Elsie Vanetti, the newspapers, for the first time, dropped the front-page story to second place. A political crisis claimed the top headline. In one paper, the Vanetti Affair was even relegated to page two.

The time had come for more stimulus, Jason decided.

He was in a cafe, eating breakfast. He had continued the habit of buying the papers and eating out, while at home Jenny was seeing to Elsie's needs.

Jason looked well. Despite the ten to twelve hours a day he had put in with Elsie, allied to the constant possibility of exposure, he bore few marks of strain. He was calm. He was confident.

This pleased and surprised him. He had fully expected beforehand to grow more tired and nervous as the days passed, as his work with the actress ground on and as the search for her intensified. In the end, it was the reverse. The manhunt was a distant baying, his sessions with Elsie were interesting and enjoyable.

Jason paid the bill, left the cafe and walked home. He stopped once on the way to buy a bunch of carnations for Jenny, who, Jason thought, needed cheering up. Over the past days she had become dull, introspective. He considered it was due to his decision about the fan club reward—to which, however, she had made no further reference.

"It's me," Jason called out at the house. Closing the door, he went up. He put the flowers behind his back.

Jenny came to the kitchen doorway. She looked pale and drawn. "Anything new?" she asked.

"No, except the story's slipping. As it was bound to."

"You'll do the scarf thing?"

"At noon, yes," Jason said. He leaned against the bannister post. "I see now, Jen, that I made a mistake leaving the purse so early in the affair."

"I don't see why."

"The story was as big as could be then. It didn't need any fuel. I wasted that purse. Wish I had it now."

"A small mistake."

"I was too eager, that's what it was. Also, I should have taken some of her money. To be sitting there, she would have had to buy something, spend. But maybe nobody knows exactly how much she had."

Jenny asked, "What've you got behind your back?"

He brought around the carnations. "Flowers."

Jenny looked at them solemnly. "Don't you think," she said, "that Elsie's in the wrong state to appreciate flowers?"

"No, Jen, they're for you. I bought them for you."

"Really?"

● ● ● ● ● ●

Jason took the Underground. His carriage had scarcely a dozen passengers—matrons going up West for lunch, their faces flushed; mothers with young children; men who had that deflated look of the unemployed.

Jason told himself he blended with the last group quite well. He wore his jeans, an old suit coat, a tieless shirt and a flat cap. His shoes, dirty, were skinned on the toe-caps like old boxing gloves.

Euston, King's Cross, Angel, Old Street, Moorgate—Jason watched the stations go by, thankful that the stop at each was brief. In spite of his general content, he was unable to keep away a growing tension.

Bank, London Bridge, Borough. The train was across the river now, in the untidy and unattractive sprawl of South London.

The train came into another station, Elephant & Castle. The doors hissed back, Jason stepped out. When passing through the barrier, he walked by a policeman without feeling a tremor.

Within ten minutes Jason was a mile from the station, walking east. From time to time, absently, he patted the pocket which held Elsie's green silk scarf. He was tense without being nervous.

On either side of the road were unglamorous factories, all old, brute buildings set closely together like toughs with their shoulders hunched.

Fronting these were people in their hundreds, men and women wearing coveralls or smocks. They talked, strolled, played cards, sat with faces tilted toward the sun. One group of men kicked a football at a goal of brickwork between two doors.

The crowd thickened as Jason came to a crossroads. Here stood a dingy pub. It was hemmed in by workers holding glasses of beer.

Jason's interest was given to two objects, both red. One was a telephone kiosk on the kerb angle near the pub, the other was a double-decker bus approaching in the distance.

Jason smiled that his timing was lucky. And as for the kiosk. He went over to check if the telephone was in working order. It was. He stayed there inside.

The bus came up. It made a sweeping, leaning U-turn at the junction and parked nearby. The driver and conductor got out, went quickly into the pub.

This point was a terminus. The bus would wait for five minutes before starting back.

Jason looked at his watch. His tension was still growing. He shared his gaze between the second hand of his watch and the bus. People were boarding sporadically.

Through the telephone booth's three glass walls came the jabber of the crowd, the clink of bottles on glasses, a tinny blare from transistor radios, the rumble of passing traffic. Jason drummed his fingers on the counter.

From the edge of his vision he saw a man walking across the road. Jason took his attention away from its two focal points to watch. The man was heading directly for the kiosk.

Jason lifted the receiver and put it to his face—that side facing the man. He moved his lips. His other hand had stopped its drumming, was holding the fingers skyward.

The man went past the kiosk and into the crowd. Jason eased down on his tension. He looked at his watch. The time was now. The bus would leave in two minutes.

He poised his forefinger and dialled, spinning the nine three times. A click, and a perky female voice asked:

"Police, Fire or Ambulance?"

"Police, please."

"Is it an emergency?"

"Yes it is. Hurry, please."

A buzzing sound followed. It went on and on, on and on. Hissing, Jason impatiently passed the receiver from one hand to the other.

A male voice said, "Police. Can I help you?"

"Listen, it's about that actress," Jason said in a gruff, urgent tone. "You know. Elsie Vanetti. She's missing. It's been in all the papers. There's a reward."

The voice was sharp. "What about her?"

"I think I've just seen her, see."

"What's your name, please?"

"She was getting on a bus at Tradeways Cross. Just now. I'm sure it's her. You'd best be lively. The bus'll be off in a minute."

"We'll see to that. Could you give me your name, please?"

"I will quick enough if it turns out I'm right. I'll be in for that reward. Bye."

"Wait a—"

Jason put down the receiver and began to push out of the door. He stopped with a gasp. Swiftly he pulled out his handkerchief, glanced through the glass to be sure he was unobserved, wiped the receiver and shelf.

Still holding the handkerchief when he stepped outside, he surreptitiously wiped the handle as he closed the door.

Don't get rattled, he cautioned himself. There's ample time. They couldn't have a car here in less than ten minutes.

He accepted that. Even so, he wanted to hurry. Resisting, he walked at a steady pace along the edge of the crowd. He kept his head lowered and slightly turned away.

Reaching the open entrance of the double-decker, he stepped up onto the platform. Faster now, he told himself. Plant the scarf and get off again.

There were fifteen or so people on the lower level. Jason went up the narrow, curving stairs. The top was empty except for four people at the favoured front.

Out of his pocket Jason took the scarf. It billowed open. He lay it in the centre of the long back seat.

From below rose a burst of talk. Jason turned and started down. Two hefty girls appeared, hustling up and chattering. The first lifted her head and called cheerily:

"Watch yourself, mate!"

After a brief hesitation, Jason reversed. At the top he went on reversing a little way along the narrow aisle.

The two girls reached the upper level. They were peroxide blondes. They wore smocks and heavy make-up. The first stopped by the back seat, saying:

"Let's sit here, May."

"Right, luv."

The girl paused. "Hey, look at that, then. Look, May, someone's left a scarf."

They stood there, crammed in the aisle, staring down at the seat. Jason moved closer. His time was running out. With face averted, he mumbled, "Excuse me."

The girls didn't hear. One said, "Looks a good 'un."

"Yeh."

"Silk, I bet."

"We'll have to turn it in."

"Turn it in?"

" 'Course."

"Don't talk bloody wet, luv."

Reproachful: "May. Don't be like that."

"Like what? Come off it. Finders keepers."

About to speak again, Jason was stopped by hearing the bus engine come to life. The vehicle began to throb.

Jason's tension swelled to an ache. He stepped quickly to the girls, turned his back to them and said loudly, "Excuse me."

Three things happened simultaneously. Feet clattered on the staircase, a bell rang, one of the girls hissed, "Grab it, grab it!"

Jason stood, irresolute and close to trembling. Elsie came into his mind.

From below appeared a man and then a woman. The two girls moved to front the seat and sat down, and Jason saw one of them stuffing the scarf into a handbag.

The bus began to move.

The man and woman reached the upper level. Jason moved back along the aisle. He was debating furiously whether it was too late to leave the bus, to get off at the next stop. Whatever excuse he tossed the conductor, he would probably be remembered.

On the other hand, if he stayed, he along with all the other passengers might be questioned by the police. That was the worst of the two.

The couple had slid into a seat. Jason went back along the aisle. The blondes were sitting squarely, one glum, the other smug.

Jason started down the stairs. He stopped. He listened.

In the distance sounded the urgent, asthmatic cry of a police car.

Jason hurried on down to the platform. The conductor was inside, far along, giving out tickets. His back was turned.

Jason moved to the platform edge. With the crook of his arm—

fingerprints in mind—he held on to the centre pole. He looked down at the roadway. It was slipping by speedily.

If he could get off without being seen . . .

The fast wheeze of the police car was louder.

Marvellously, the bus began to slow. Jason swung out and looked ahead. They were approaching a stop, where a man was holding up his arm.

Jason got himself in a forward-facing position. Then, twenty yards from the stop, he stepped down. His feet hit the road, he was flung forward by impetus, he ran and waved his arms; and he held his balance.

Stepping over the kerb, he began to walk back the other way.

This area was a match for that beyond the pub: factories, scores of people. Jason moved in from the roadway and reduced his walk to a stroll, feeling safe among the workers.

He was beginning to settle from his alarm. So much so that he gave up for a moment worrying about himself to curse at the thought that the scarf was lost, wasted. All that danger for nothing.

The police siren racketed. A moment later, the car itself flashed by in pursuit of the bus. The factory workers stared and made jokes about cops and robbers.

Jason walked on. He didn't like the fact that he was headed for the junction. The police would certainly go there, if they weren't there already in another car, for they would be sure to deduce that the anonymous call had come from the kiosk. But there was nothing he could do about it.

Jason twitched nervously as from close by sounded the blast of a whistle. The shrill cry was taken up by other whistles along the straight road.

The people started to move. They were drawn toward doors like filings to a magnet. The whistles stopped.

In one minute, the road was empty.

Jason dawdled to a halt. He felt horribly vulnerable. He looked both ways. Apart from himself, there was only one person in the area, a man collecting bottles and glasses outside the pub.

In the other direction, Jason could see, faintly, the red double-decker. It was standing still.

A police-car cry began.

Jason didn't hesitate. He went to the nearest doorway and stepped inside. There was a long, concrete passage. At hand, an older man was sweeping. He looked up enquiringly.

Jason asked, "Er—any jobs going?"

The man shrugged. "Dunno. You could try. Personnel manager, his office is at the end there. Second door around the corner."

"Thanks."

"Unskilled, is it?"

"Yes."

"Not a hope, lad."

"I'll try anyway," Jason said. He went on.

At the end of the passage, facing the left turn, was a door. Jason glanced back. The old man was involved in his sweeping. Jason opened the door and went through.

He was in an alley. He followed it. From windows on either side came a hum of machinery. The alley opened out into a cindered yard. There were baby mountains of scrap metal. Sheets of iron were being unloaded from a truck.

The police siren was somewhere close.

Jason went on, walking at a brisk pace. The men at the truck gave him only a casual glance. He reached a massive gateway. Through it he was on a street. He quickened his step, then broke into a jog.

Twice he turned corners onto others streets. The next turn brought him onto a main road. There were houses, small shops, and people standing at a bus stop.

Jason slowed back to a walk. There was no sound of a police car. He went to join the waiting people.

● ● ● ● ● ●

The next day, Saturday, Jason broke his routine of going out to eat and buy the papers. He wanted to get straight to work with Elsie, make up for an indifferent afternoon and evening the day before, when post-excitement lethargy and the scarf failure had allowed him to let Elsie ramble over unimportant ground.

The three of them took breakfast at the dining table. Elsie ate like a robot, Jenny was the silent person she had become lately, Jason mulled over his notes for the coming session. The clink of cutlery formed the only sound.

Afterwards, Jenny went out and Jason took the actress into her room. She sat, as instructed, on the chair, which now was positioned by the bedfoot. Sitting or lounging there, Jason could pat Elsie's arm or hold her hand. Anytime he felt like it, he could hold her hand.

After sending Elsie into a deep trance, which took just over a minute, Jason set to work.

An hour later he was lying back comfortably, relaxed as always when here. He had stopped giving his full attention to Elsie, who was talking about an early boyfriend. His thoughts were on the last subject they had covered: charities.

Being without modesty in her trance state, Elsie had spoken freely of her charity work. There had been appeals, picketings which could have been damaging to her popularity, personal appearances at functions and the openings of bazaars, membership of committees, flag selling. All of which had taken valuable time; time that was money. Additionally, there had been her own donations.

Jason felt proud, which he thought ridiculous. Next he felt remiss, which he thought absurd.

He felt remiss for his lack of higher purpose. He was risking prison simply for gold and self-glory. The criminality and, yes, the immorality, they could be semi-forgiven if he were striving for an unselfish goal; if, for instance, he intended using his coming fame and money to further the cause of hypnotism. The still-fledgling science needed dedicated men. He could be one of them.

Discomforted, Jason thought how stupidly his mind worked at times. He sat up, took Elsie's hand and listened as she talked.

Soon he asked, "Was he your first lover?"

"Lover? Well, yes."

"I mean, did you become intimate with him? Sexual intercourse?"

Elsie shook her head, smiling quietly. "I didn't want to, not with John. I did later, with—with someone else. I can't remember his name."

Nor what he looked like or anything connected with him, Jason thought. That boyfriend he had eradicated from her mind.

"But you didn't," he stated.

"No, I didn't ever, not until . . ." She broke off, looking at Jason for help.

He knew she meant Hull Rainer, and Rainer was forgotten. "It doesn't matter, dear. Let's get back to John. Can you picture him clearly?"

The morning wore on. Elsie talked, Jason expunged.

It occurred to him that it was about time he tested the power of his control. This would relate to the longevity of her memory-loss. There were several tests he could use. Apropos of the earlier talk, he chose one in the field of love.

The main schism in hypnotism was whether an entranced subject could be made to commit an act which, awake, he would not countenance. One camp said yes, the other no. Both were vehement. Empirical evidence was difficult to come by. If a subject was actually made to, say, steal, there was no way of knowing if he would not be prepared to do so normally.

Jason got off the bed and told Elsie to stand up. He moved close.

"Elsie," he said. "You are with a stranger. He is attractive but you have never seen him before. He has followed you along the street, talked to you, picked you up. It is nighttime. You are both standing in a doorway. He has asked you for a kiss. Do you understand?"

She nodded. He said, "Kiss the stranger, Elsie."

Her hesitation was brief. She lifted her face, reaching with her lips. Jason bent down. They kissed.

Jason was moved by a curious sensation. He was unable to judge if it were embarrassment, annoyance with himself for taking this advantage, exhilaration at success, or something else. He did know he felt distinctly unsettled.

Breaking off the kiss abruptly, he said a curt, "Lie on the bed and rest." He left the room.

Jenny looked around from wiping the tabletop. "You're finished early."

"I need a break."

"There was nothing new in the papers, by the way. The scarf wasn't mentioned."

Jason nodded absently. Jenny said, "The police apparently are answering dozens of false alarms every day. That's what they'd think the scarf thing was."

"I'm going for a walk," Jason said. "Then I'll have a bite out. See you later."

● ● ● ● ● ●

His walk was short. He soon recovered his emotional balance, deciding that his feelings with Elsie had been due to success, even though the test had been frail—and he wondered why he had chosen it.

Not hungry enough to eat, Jason set off back. He wanted to be home.

It was odd, Jason thought, how lately he had come to think of Number Nine as a home. Before, it had simply been a place to live, a place without charm. He supposed the change was due to the threat from outside implied by the situation. It gave the flat that allure of safety.

It was quiet in Shank Place. A toddler, tethered to a portico pillar with rope, was pulling hairs from a doll's head. The legs of a baby kicked up from within a hoodless pram. The sun was offensive to the moribund houses and cars.

Jason crossed the road. He went up the steps of Number Nine, unlocked the door and stepped inside. He called, "I'm back!"

Something was wrong.

Jason, pausing with his hand on the door, could sense that. Or thought he could. It was the atmosphere. The silence.

He called, "Jenny?"

No answer.

"Jenny?"

No answer. The silence went on.

Jason closed the door, and, not knowing why, did so quietly. He went to the foot of the stairs. She's asleep, he told himself. He believed it partially.

Halfway up the staircase he called Jenny again. The name echoed back at him and in the trip acquired an essence of mock.

By the bannister post on the landing he stopped. He gazed around. His tension of the scarf danger was back, and more acute than yesterday. Then he had known the why of it.

He felt cold inside, as if he had drunk his fill of ice water. The hand on the post was slippery with sweat.

"Jenny?"

He winced at the harshness in his voice.

No answer.

Jason went to the front-bedroom door and flung it open. The bed, neatly made, was empty. He went into the room. No one was there.

Back on the landing he strode along to the other door. With his hand on the knob, Jason hesitated. He didn't want to know. He was horrified at the idea of having his suspicion verified.

It couldn't be, he thought, and even hated to give the thought its freedom. It was impossible. Jenny taking Elsie away in order to claim the reward? No, not possible.

He turned the knob and gently pushed the door back, right back against the wall. The room was empty. Feeling weak, Jason went in at a slow pace.

He looked at the bed. He looked at the chair where Elsie always sat. His chest ached. He rubbed it absently with both hands while continuing to gaze around. His tension had gone. He felt sad, beaten.

Moving at the same crawling pace to the bed, Jason stared at the pillow's centre indentation. He leaned over and touched it with his fingertips.

His physical weakness grew. He turned and sat heavily on the mattress. His body slumped, back convexing. His mouth slackened. He stared at the wall.

A crash sounded.

Jason jerked to his feet as if pulled by a wire. The crash he recognised. It had been the closing of the front door.

"Who's there?" he called, running from the room. "Who is it?" He dashed to the head of the stairs.

There he halted, swaying and staring down.

Below stood Elsie Vanetti.

She stood looking up at him. She wore raincoat, scarf, sunglasses, shoes. She was exactly as she had been when he had taken her away from the theatre.

They stared at one another in silence. Jason's face twisted at the weirdness of it all.

Some time passed before he found himself thinking: The scarf. It's wrong. She can't possibly have the scarf.

Elsie spoke. She had Jenny's voice. She asked nervously, "Are you angry?"

"What?"

Jenny took off the dark glasses. "Darling, I—"

One fist clenched and raised, Jason shouted, "Where's Elsie?"

"In the bath. The poor thing, I couldn't—"

Jason whirled, went to the bathroom and yanked the door open. He sagged with a shuddery sigh of relief. Elsie was kneeling passively in deep water, her back turned.

Slowly Jason drew the door to its jamb.

The sound of quick footsteps. Jenny appeared at his side. "Darling," she said. "I'm sorry. I didn't expect you home for an hour yet."

He felt dazed. "What?"

"I'm sorry about the bath. She needed one so badly."

Jason turned to her. "It's okay," he said, tired again.

He saw now that the scarf was not, of course, Elsie's; this was a lighter green. The coat too, though similar, was not the one which had been so widely publicised. And the shoes and sunglasses, they also belonged to Jenny.

He asked, "What's it all about?"

"I wanted to help," Jenny said. She put her arms around his waist and rested her head on his chest. "I've been such a bitch to you. And you were so sweet yesterday. The flowers."

"Help?"

"Keep the affair hot. You know."

Jason nodded, frowning. "Tell me where you've been."

"Just out. Walking around. Lots of people looked at me. I'll bet they thought I was the real thing. It'll be talked about, you see. And then the press might pick it up. Elsie Vanetti seen in Camden Town. That kind of thing."

Jason had become fully alert. His voice was hard. "You've been walking around near here?"

Jenny drew back. She flinched. "Well, yes. Yes, dear."

"I don't believe it. You can't be that stupid."

"Jason."

"Don't you see what you've done?"

"No."

He stared at her. "They'll call the police. Someone's bound to call. You may have been followed. They could be on their way here now, this minute."

"No, Jason," Jenny said. She looked close to tears.

"Yes, Jenny," he snapped. "There's twenty-five thousand pounds at stake."

Putting her hands to her mouth, she whispered, "I was only trying to help."

Jason swung away. Then he stopped. He said, "Listen!"

Faintly, he could hear the yammer of a police car. He stood still, straining to gauge direction and volume. He succeeded. The sound was coming closer.

"Police," he said.

Jenny: "Could be an ambulance."

"Police."

"Could be a fire engine."

"Police."

"But they might not be coming here, Jason. Darling. We're always hearing that noise."

He ran into the front bedroom. In the bay he looked out at the street. It appeared to be the same as before. He could hear the siren clearer from here. The volume was still growing.

Jason hurried back to Jenny. He said, "Put the glasses on. Go out. Walk away."

"What?"

"You heard. Walk away."

"Where?"

"Just away. If that is the police, and if they are looking for you— let them find you. Understand? Let them see the mistake. Understand?"

Jenny looked afraid and tearful as she put the sunglasses back on.

The siren was piercingly loud.

Jason took Jenny's arm and hurried her down the stairs. He pulled the door open, saying, "Quick. Get away from here."

Jenny went outside and down the steps. Jason closed the door. He charged upstairs three steps at a time and went into the front room and looked out of the window.

What he saw made him gasp and draw back.

At the end of the street, a police car was stopping.

Jason moved to the window frame and peered around its edge. He saw Jenny walking. He saw the car's occupants, two uniformed officers, get out and stand watching the approaching girl. He saw, in effect, the end of his plan and of his dreams.

Jenny was about to walk past the policemen. One of them gestured. She stopped. She took off her dark glasses and drew down the headscarf. One officer, the driver, went around the car and got back inside. The other man went on talking. He put his hands on his hips. Jenny was shaking her head. The policeman turned away and got in the car, which then drove off. Jenny walked on. She went from sight.

Jason moved to the bed, let himself drop onto it face down, closed his eyes, sighed. He told himself it might be all right. It might, it might.

Presently, he heard the front door close. He got up torpidly and went out to the landing. As he was sitting on the couch, Jenny appeared at the stairhead. She too had been moving slowly.

"It wasn't anything," Jenny said, face blank. "They said it was the fourth today. Vanetti-sighting, they called it. They asked my name. I gave them a false name and address, but they weren't listening anyway."

"It sounds good, Jen," Jason said emptily. He felt drained.

"The policeman who stayed, he was nasty. He said half the young girls in London were going round in raincoats, sunglasses and green scarves. It's all the rage. And he asked if I wasn't a bit old for that kind of nonsense."

Jason said, "I'm sorry I shouted at you."

Jenny shrugged one shoulder, as if the apology were a hand there. "You had every right. What I did was stupid."

"You were only trying to help."

"I could've ruined the whole thing. Maybe I have."

"I don't know."

"Will this be bad later, when you go forward?"

"I'll have to think about it. But not now."

Jenny took off her coat. She asked, "Did you eat?"

"No."

"I'll fix you something."

"Not hungry," Jason said. "Only tired." He lowered himself sideways onto the couch. "Very tired."

● ● ● ● ● ●

Later that night, Jenny went out to get the Sunday newspapers, which were always available in the West End an hour or so before midnight on Saturdays. She was keen to read the piece which had been advertised during the week: "My Life With Elsie" by Hull Rainer.

Jason changed into pyjamas and went to bed. Earlier, after a nap, he had spent a solid six hours with the actress. Perhaps because of the emergency, he had worked with severe diligence.

Propped up on pillows, Jason mused on the future, near and far, as it concerned the disappearance of Miss Elsie Vanetti. Near meant a replacement factor for the scarf—and Jason again fumed at the girl who had stolen it; next, at himself for having wasted the purse, whose contents he could have dropped one at a time.

He would have to use the raincoat, he thought. It was chancy, for the police would wonder how she hadn't caught a cold or worse, spending nights in the open while wearing only a light dress. But the weather was warm, and it may be assumed she had slept in old buildings, and in any case there would not be many nights now before she was returned.

Which led to future far. Once he had introduced himself into the affair, Jason wondered, Would the police connect the man from

Shank Place with the Vanetti-dressed girl seen there? It was possible. A suspicion, however, was not proof. Also, if his address wasn't published, the two officers from today could hardly make the suspect connexion—even if they recalled that one incident out of many. Moving after releasing Elsie would be a mistake. A brand-new abode would seem curious.

Jason concluded that the odds were in his favour.

He closed his eyes and dozed. He dreamed. He saw himself on the stage of a vast auditorium, in white tie and tails. The audience sat enraptured by his art. The watching Jason was surprised by the lack of satisfaction in the dream Jason's face.

He awoke to a call of, "I'm home!"

A moment later, Jenny came in and tossed him the newspapers. She said, "No mention of today. Only that the police are still being called to false alarms."

"Good. We're off the front page, I see."

"But the story's still big, if not actually news. The *Sunday Times* magazine has the Vanetti story in pictures, and the *Observer* has a piece on Elsie as an actress, written by four famous directors."

"Favourable?"

"Very," Elsie said, taking off her coat.

After looking at the magazine photographs, Jason picked up the *Sunday Standard*. He started to read "My Life With Elsie."

"Good God," he said.

"Mm?"

"*The first time my eyes rested on this slim, beautiful girl, I felt something happen in my deepest heart.* Good God."

"It *is* a bit icky," Jenny said.

"Icky? It stinks." He read on. After two paragraphs he tossed the paper aside roughly. "What bloody awful gush."

Jenny raised her eyebrows at him. "There's no need to get so violent, dear."

"Bloody rubbish."

"It's no skin off your nose, Jason."

"I know that. It's the cheapness I'm angry about."

Jenny picked up her bathrobe and went to the door. Before going out she said, "You're blind, darling."

10

Hull Rainer got up at eleven o'clock on Sunday morning. Humming, he washed, shaved with care, spent some minutes getting his hair the way he liked it.

He put on a scarlet dressing gown and admired himself in the mirror. Young, he thought. Young and vital. Juvenile lead on the climb.

Moving closer to the glass, his pleasure held, Hull searched the planes of his face. He wondered for the hundredth time, and dismissed with equal frequency, if it were true what some people said: that sex drains youth. That, therefore, his pick-ups, with their irresistibly smooth bodies, could be slowly but surely making him old before his time.

Hull's laugh was not totally at ease as he turned away. He went into the kitchen and fixed coffee. When it was ready he brought in the newspapers.

His ghosted piece on Elsie was enjoyable, even moving in places. He read it twice before turning to the football results and other items and, last, barrel-scraping, aspects of the Vanetti Affair.

The telephone rang.

Hull sighed. He assumed the call to be the police making their regular check for news. To hell with them, he thought.

Other calls, that stream had become a dribble during the past days. Interest was flagging. No longer were reporters hanging around the front of the building. Friends had stopped asking and advising and sympathising. Hull regretted the downward trend.

In Hull's career, however, the movement was up. George Case had been approached by the producer of a road-show play, had accepted for Hull a guest spot on a TV quiz programme one month hence, was keeping on the dangle an advertising agency that had ideas of using Hull in various sponsorships.

As for *The Road Turns Back*, Hull had returned the screenplay with an enthusiastic cover note . . .

He sat up straight, as it occured to him that the still-ringing telephone could be a call from Samuel Finegold.

He hurried to the living room and lifted the receiver.

A woman's voice said, "Mr Rainer? This is Madam de Paton. You may be familiar with my name."

"I'm afraid not."

"I'm a spiritualist, Mr Rainer. A sensitive. A medium. One of the most gifted in this country, though I do say so myself."

"And?"

"Mr Rainer, last night I dreamt of your wife. She was in a large boxlike construction. She was alive and seemed happy and—"

"Lady," Hull said, "I saw that movie too."

"I beg your pardon?"

Hull stopped himself when on the point of terminating the call. It had come to him that soon he might find it useful, or necessary, to have the Vanetti Affair back in full prominence. Something exotic would be needed. What more so than a seance? It had the right newsworthy flavour. Dramatic figures in a darkened room trying to contact the missing actress.

Hull said, "Madam de Paton, it was good of you to ring up and tell me this. As it happens, I'm busy at the moment with another line of investigation, but perhaps I'll contact you if this doesn't meet with success. Could I have your number, please?"

The woman obliged and went on eagerly about her dream: Elsie had been as she appeared in the police picture except for scarf and sunglasses; she had been sitting quietly on a chair; her hair was untidy.

Hull heard the nonsense out. He thanked Madam de Paton politely before ringing off.

Back with the newspapers, he turned to the theatre section. Here too he found Elsie mentioned. At the foot of a column was, *Out of a sense of duty to the understudy-makes-hit fiction, I went to see the Vanetti play again. Alas, Miss Adele Walden, though nice to look at, lacks the maturity this role demands. It will be interesting to see what producer Roger Burn does next.*

Hull went to the telephone and dialled Burn's number. Money was at stake. The highly favourable contract called for Miss Vanetti to go on half salary should she be incapacitated, regardless of how long that state should last.

If, Hull thought, Burn decided to take the play off, a pretty sum of free money would be lost.

A woman answered. "Oh hello, Hull. Roger's not in. He went to the theatre."

"On Sunday?"

"It's that Walden girl. She's not working out. Roger's putting her through her paces this morning. But he's not at all happy."

Hull chatted for a minute, rang off and went to dress.

● ● ● ● ● ●

The West End was quiet. Only public transport moved along Shaftesbury Avenue. Everything was shuttered and dead.

Hull parked beside the theatre. He went along the alley, across the yard sided with scenery, up the steps and through the unguarded door. Backstage was dim. From ahead came light and a girl's voice.

Hull went along a corridor, through the stalls bar and into the auditorium. Roger Burn was sitting in the front row. Above him, on the lighted stage, stood a girl. She stopped speaking as Hull approached.

Burn's greeting was gloomy. A tall man in rumpled clothes, he had a long jaw and a nose like a fist.

He gestured. "You two met?"

"No," Hull said. "Hello, darling."

"How do you do, Mr Rainer."

Adele Walden was petite. She wore a simple black dress. Her sweet-pretty face was enclosed by long, dark hair. She stood with her hands moving nervously in and out of a clasp.

Delicious, Hull thought. Frightened and delicious.

He said, "Don't let me interrupt anything."

"We're just about finished," Roger Burn said. "Sit down. Adele dear, go and smoke a cigarette or something."

"Yes, Mr Burn," the girl said. She wandered offstage.

Hull sat beside the producer. "You look blue, old son."

"This kid, she's got ability all right, but she's not for this part. Her big scene at the end, she plays it like Peter Pan."

"Someone else? A name?"

Burn shook his head. "Paying half salary to Elsie, we can't afford a name."

"Tell me, Roger, how's the box office?"

"Couldn't be better, as it happens."

Hull spread his hands. "So what's the strife?"

"Did you get the review this morning? A few more like that, plus word of mouth, and we start getting cancellations. At the moment, it's the notoriety that's bringing 'em in."

"Listen," Hull said, lying glibly. "I caught the play the other night. Queued like a peasant and went up to the gods. And you know, Adele isn't bad. Not bad at all. Hell, an old girl next to me, she was in tears."

"Yes?"

"Absolutely."

The producer shook his head again. He did it smoothly, was obviously practiced. "But this kid's so damned nervous."

"She'll settle down."

"She's done the play twelve times," Burn said. "And it's not so much that, anyway—it's Wilkinson."

"The cop?"

"That same charmer. He's been here three or four times. Adele's convinced he thinks she did away with Elsie so she could have the part."

"Balls," Hull said. "Elsie's up to some silly game of her own."

"That's what I think as well. It fits."

Hull looked at him. "Fits?"

"You know. With the way Elsie's been behaving."

Hull said, "Wilkinson mentioned that. I thought it was just stupid talk."

The producer folded his arms and leaned away. "You mean you hadn't noticed the change in Elsie?"

"No."

"Everyone else did. For the past two months now she's been very odd. Highly strung at times, like a zombie at others. I thought she was ill. Maybe she is."

Hindsight exaggeration, Hull thought. He said, "Elsie's all right. She'll turn up one of these days. She'll be furious if you fold. She might even sue."

"Elsie wouldn't do that to me."

"You'd be wise to keep going as long as you've got full houses."

Burn sighed. "I suppose. We'll let it ride for the time being." He looked at his watch. "Must away. I've done what I could with Adele."

"Look, Roger," Hull said earnestly. "Let me have a gab with her. I'll settle her mind about Wilkinson. I'll also tell her how Elsie sees this part, her feelings on it." He added, lying again, "Elsie talked to me a lot about this role."

A minute later, Roger Burn had gone and Hull was climbing over the footlights. He went into the wings. Adele Walden, sitting on a prop couch, looked around quickly.

She said a brittle, "Hello."

"Hi."

"Where's Mr Burn?"

"Gone."

The girl asked, tautly, "What's the verdict, Mr Rainer?"

"Mm?"

"Am I in or out?"

Carefully, Hull said, "As a matter of fact, darling, he left the final decision up to me. I'm a sort of stand-in for my wife. As you know, she has choice of supporting cast."

"Yes."

Hull sat beside her. He was stirred by her smallness and femininity and her large, frightened eyes.

"You feel happy in the part, sweet?"

Avidly: "Oh yes, Mr Rainer. It's a marvellous part. This is the biggest thing that's ever happened to me. I do hope you think I'm satisfactory. Shall I go through my big speech for you?"

"No, that's okay. Let me tell you my wife's feelings."

Hull extemporised. He had a fervent audience.

"Do you see what I mean, darling?"

"Yes, Mr Rainer, I think so."

"Look," Hull said. "It's dreary here. Let's go to my place and have a drink."

Adele Walden looked away. Her manner was wary. She said, "Actually, I'm meeting my boyfriend for lunch."

Shrugging, Hull got up. "As you wish."

The girl also rose. "But I can call him up and cancel."

"You do that, sweet. You just do that."

After using a backstage telephone, Adele left with Hull. They got in the car. During the drive to Lancaster Gate, Hull gave his marriage-of-convenience story and brought up the subject of Chief Inspector Wilkinson.

"He's working on a new line. He's satisfied now that Elsie's disappearance is unconnected with the theatre."

"Truly?"

"Yes. I saw him this morning."

Adele smiled. "Gosh, that's an awful relief. I was sure he had it in for me."

"So now you've got only one problem, sweet. Do you or do you not keep the part."

Adele said a quiet, "Yes."

At the flat, Hull poured two whiskies. He sat on a couch facing Adele on another of the foursome. Small talk accompanied the drinking of the whisky.

Hull put down his glass. He said, "How badly do you want to stay on in the play, darling?"

A blush came on the girl's neck and rose to her face. She looked into her empty glass, saying, "Very badly."

"I see."

There was a pause. Hull waited. Finally the girl said, still looking down, "May I ask you a direct question?"

"Of course."

Another pause before, "Is this a casting-couch situation?"

Hull smiled. "Yes, darling."

The girl looked up. Her blush had faded. That frightened air was back. Tonelessly she asked, "What do you want me to do?"

Hull said, "Go in the bedroom and take your clothes off."

"Yes, Mr Rainer," the girl said. She rose and left the room.

11

Jason, walking along Oxford Street on Monday morning, felt uneasy. He was not going to take any chances on having the raincoat stolen or go astray, which meant taking greater chances to guarantee success.

As always during shopping hours, Oxford Street was as crowded as an Eastern bazaar. The packed, slow-moving traffic formed an odd contrast to the bustle on the sidewalks. People shoved in and out of the large stores, bunched at crossings, strode along in the gutter to make better time.

It was a colourful, sunlit scene. Clothing ranged from saris to stetsons, and the least-heard language was English—tourists, the foreign colony and Continental shoppers outnumbering the natives. Street musicians entertained on the kerbs. Peddlers of junk opened shop from a suitcase while partners kept watch for patrolling constables.

To Jason it was all a comforting density. He moved at a comparatively slow pace on the inside of the pavement. Under his arm was a paper sack containing Elsie Vanetti's coat.

Jason wore windcheater and round-neck sweater, jeans and the old felt hat. As an extra precaution he had put on his false beard. He believed he looked fairly average; or at least, ordinary enough when seen among the more exotically arrayed.

Jason's uneasiness was for what lay ahead. It increased now like a growing ache as he turned in at the wide entrance of a department store.

Here he still had the comfort of dense bustle, but the moment for him to act was drawing closer.

He moved along an aisle between counters. Noticing a salesgirl look at him as he went by, Jason realised his face was set and showing the strain. He tried for a casual expression.

The aisle widened into a square. In the centre stood a four-sided counter. Tending it was a woman with blue-rinse hair and spectacles of thick black frames. She appeared, Jason assured himself, suitably efficient.

Above the counter a sign said INFORMATION, and in smaller print LOST PROPERTY. Three people were there: a couple and a man in a turban.

Jason had stopped by a display of bedroom slippers. He needed to choose his moment with care. If the information woman had too many people to deal with, she might be inattentive. If she had no one, her attention could be acute—for the hander-in of the lost object as well as the object itself.

Jason watched from the corners of his eyes. The man in the turban left. He was replaced at once by three teen-age girls. A voice close to Jason asked, "Can I help you?"

Glancing up from under the brim of his hat, he saw a salesgirl. She was leaning toward him from over the slippers.

He said, "Just browsing, thank you."

The girl moved away.

At the centre counter, the couple was leaving. Jason urged himself not to hesitate. Delay was dangerous. For his own part, he could only grow more edgy; in respect of others, they would begin to notice the loitering man.

Well shielded by the display before him and the passing crowd at his back, Jason pulled the raincoat out of the bag. The coat was folded in readiness, its label prominent.

There were still only the three girls at the information desk. Jason moved across. He held the raincoat in one hand, the empty paper bag in the other.

The blue-haired woman was explaining how to get to the pet department. She glanced around as Jason came up.

Head down, as if he were looking at the coat as he put it on the counter, Jason said in broken English:

"I find this over there. On stairs."

"Thank you," the woman said, interrupting and going back to her directions to the girls.

Jason turned away. He was wide-eyed with relief. Never had he imagined it would be that simple. He had expected at least to be asked to leave a name.

He glanced back. The girls were going and the woman, the efficient woman, she was staring at the raincoat's label.

Quickening his step, Jason moved on. He put two aisles between himself and the information desk. A jostle from someone in the crowd made him aware of the paper sack he still carried.

Absently, he folded the bag and shoved it inside his open windcheater and held it there. He hurried on.

From behind him a firm voice said, "Excuse me."

Jason felt a surge of alarm. He was about to go even faster, but a hand took hold of his arm. He was pulled to a halt.

The owner of the hand stood beside him. The man was Jason's age and height but thirty pounds heavier. He had a crewcut and a hard, unsmiling face.

"Excuse me," he said again.

"What?" Jason mumbled. He was aware that shoppers had stopped to watch.

The man asked, "Would you mind showing me what's under your jacket?"

"I—I don't understand."

The man lifted his free hand to the lapel of his suit and turned it over. Beneath was a plastic card with printing and a photograph.

He said, "Security."

Christ, Jason thought, he thinks I'm a shoplifter. It was the speed and the hidden hand.

The floorwalker said, "Perhaps it might be better if we stepped over there where it's quiet."

Jason panicked. He could see himself being questioned, which, while in itself innocuous, would mean time—time for his face to be firmly registered in the man's mind.

Abruptly, Jason gave a huge shove.

The restraining hand lost its grip, the floorwalker went staggering back. Jason charged on.

He leapt at the ring of hovering watchers. They scattered in strides or falters. One man made a lunging grab, missed, fell to his knees.

Jason ran on along the aisle. He could hear on the woodstrip flooring two sets of pounding feet. People ahead turned at the noise. He pushed past them roughly. The paper sack fell from under his jacket.

He swung around into another aisle. Without looking back fully, he could see the crewcut man close behind, two yards away. Everywhere there were cries of surprise and voices raised in question.

Ahead, a youth was standing. He watched with open mouth. In a gesture more defensive than capturing, he raised both hands.

Jason reached the youth. He grabbed him, twisted around and flung him back behind.

The floorwalker and the youth collided. The latter fell with a cry. The security man was delayed by a precious two seconds.

Jason sped on. He went in an ungainly spread-armed lurch around the bend of another aisle. His hat fell off.

He reached for it. His scrabbling fingers missed by half an inch. He let the hat go and ran on.

At the end of the aisle—an exit. The wide doorway was empty. Beyond lay the sunlit street. Jason forced his body to greater speed, gritting his teeth in a snarl.

Suddenly the aisle was blocked. Across it had been swung a large hamper on wheels. The hamper was chest-high with boxes. These a man in a smock began putting on a counter.

Jason went on. He flung himself up and onto the pile. Boxes went scattering. The man shouted. A hand grabbed Jason's ankle. He kicked free as he was getting clumsily to his feet. The kick made him lose his balance.

He fell sideways onto the counter top.

Toys there clanked and tinkled and cracked. Jason rolled. He dropped into the narrow walkway between counters. A salesgirl held her temples and screamed.

Jason got up, pushed by her and chased on.

He could hear other screams, also shouts. He felt like screaming himself. He felt like dropping in a heap and giving up. The desire to get away was stronger.

He jumped up onto the counter, crunched plastic toys, jumped to the floor and raced toward the doorway. A fast glance behind showed him the crewcut man leaping down from the hamper.

Jason clenched his teeth, wheeled his arms. If he could get outside, dodge through the traffic, cut off into back streets . . .

Into the doorway from outside surged a group of women. Fat and ponderous, they were talking excitedly in French.

Jason was unable to stop. Making an abortive turn, he crashed into the group side-on. He slipped to one knee. The shrieks above him were deafening.

He got up. Right there, reaching, was the man with the crewcut. His face was twisted with determination and rage.

Jason swung a punch of desperation. An uppercut, he brought it mightily from low on his hip. It caught the man a glancing blow on the cheek. He staggered back with a harsh gasp.

There was another man. He was approaching, pushing fast through shoppers. He bore the same stamp as the other.

Jason turned and ran. His lungs were heaving.

The way was clear. People had moved to the area of excitement Jason had just quitted. Stared at by salesgirls, he ran along aisles. A jumble of running footsteps sounded from behind.

He came to an escalator. There were people on it. He lept on and forged his way up. Anyone who moved out of the standing side he shoved back. He left a trail of angry calls.

The escalator's final third was vacant. He ran up freely. Turning at the top, he found himself in calm. Shoppers moved among racks of clothing. He slowed to a walk.

From below he heard the voice of the crewcut man shouting, "Make way! Emergency!"

Jason steeled himself against the urge to run. He must do nothing that would attract attention. Closing his gaping, air-craving mouth, he breathed heavily through his nose.

He went deeper into the clothing racks. A swelling in the murmur of talk told him the two security men had reached this floor. He went on, keeping to the steady pace.

He saw a door marked FIRE EXIT. Glancing around, seeing no one, he went to it swiftly. Through it he was on a landing. Stone steps went up and down. He chose to go up.

Climbing, he ripped off his beard. He stuffed it in his jeans pocket. Next he took off his windcheater. He balled it and threw it ahead of him up the stairs. By the time he had reached that point, he had removed his sweater.

He bunched the sweater and threw it ahead. He put on and zipped up the windcheater. He picked up his sweater and pulled it on. He flipped into view his shirt collar. He was vaguely astonished at how clearly he was thinking.

Another landing, another door. Jason pushed through. A salesgirl stood nearby. She was interested in her fingernails. Jason walked on.

Camping equipment gave way to fishing tackle. An archway disguised as a bower led to domestic pets: cages, pens, fish tanks, a zoo smell. Three teen-age girls were looking at birdcages.

Jason strolled. His ears were tuned for sounds of chase. He was persuading himself his position was good. One, they would have expected him to go down, not up. Two, his appearance was changed. Three, they wouldn't guard all the exits for a mere suspected shoplifter. Four, the lost hat was untraceable to him. Five, there was no reason for anyone to assume a connexion between the shoplifter and the lost raincoat.

But that coat, he realised, would be bringing the police.

Jason had reached the stack of birdcages. He stood there beside the three girls, who were arguing happily over what size they should get.

Jason caught a glimpse of movement. Turning his head slightly, he saw the second security man. He was coming through the archway.

To the nearest girl Jason said, "My daughter's about your age. What colour cage do you think she'd like?"

All the girls answered. Each said a different colour. Jason leaned closer, saying, "You think so?" and, "Why's that?"

The sweeping gaze of the security man rested on the group, moved on. He walked away and out of sight.

"I'd better ask her," Jason said. "Thanks."

He strolled off. Back through the arch he found a flight of stairs. He went down at a casual pace. The next flight led to the ground floor.

Everything below appeared normal. A different woman now stood at the information desk. There were no signs of the crewcut man or his colleague. The three exits visible seemed to be unguarded.

Jason walked toward the main door. He looked about him as if with interest at the displayed goods. No one paid him any heed.

He reached the doorway, shuffled through it with the crowd, got outside, and strode away.

● ● ● ● ● ●

Full calm did not return to Jason until late that afternoon. He became relaxed only toward the end of a long session with Elsie. Her voice and her memoirs brought him peace. The latter especially, as always, gave him a satisfaction which defied definition.

Could be, he had thought, that the recollections of childhood and youth, being so much more halcyon than his own, made him pretend he was their owner. The same with later bounds from one career success to another. Could be that all the recounted stories were gratifyingly free from ugliness; there was such a continuing theme of innocence. Could be that everything combined to present a picture of a woman who was decent, kind, tolerant, honest—attributes he had admired, though sometimes with embarrassment for his old-fashionedness, and now admired more and without the mental blush.

Alternately lying back to listen and sitting up to hold Elsie's hand while giving her instructions, Jason worked until Jenny announced with a tap on the door that supper was ready.

It took less than a minute to change Elsie's trance from profound to preliminary. She lost her light animation and became the open-eyed somnambulist. Her body slumped inside the plain grey dress.

"Come, dear," Jason said. "Time to eat."

When all three were seated at the dining table, Jenny, ladling out stew, said, "It hasn't been mentioned yet. Radio or TV." There was no feeling in her voice.

Jason shrugged. "It will be."

"It couldn't be another flop, could it?"

"No. I told you. The woman looked at the label. Later, she'd gone."

"But it could still be a flop," Jenny said in a capable tone.

"I suppose."

"Then what?"

Jason smiled at her. Never, he thought, would he understand women. At the beginning of this affair, Jenny had been nervous and carping. Next she had become sullen. Next came a burst of enthusiasm. Now she was as matter-of-fact as a nurse, one who behaves as if, serious though the patient might be, she herself is not emotionally involved.

Jason said, "If the coat doesn't work out, that means conclusion."

"Take Elsie back?"

"Yes. She's just about ready anyway."

"When?" Jenny asked. "When will you take her back? Tomorrow?"

Jason took his time about saying, "Well, no. I'd need tomorrow for final tests and so on. The day after." He nodded. "But the raincoat will be okay."

"We'll know after the TV news tonight," Jenny said blandly. "Pass the bread, please."

The meal continued in silence.

Afterwards, with Elsie on her bed and covered with a blanket,

Jason worked on the shoes while Jenny went out for the final edition of the evening newspapers.

Jason rubbed the soles carefully on the brick. They were so thin now in the centre that a rough thrust could make a hole. That would mean there should be a corresponding soreness or cut on Elsie's foot, which Jason had no intention of creating. He worked close to the welt.

When Jenny returned, she tossed him a paper with, "Page two."

The item consisted of three lines under the heading COAT FOUND. It said that a raincoat of the type worn by Elsie Vanetti, the missing actress, had been found today in Selfways department store.

Disappointed, Jason said, "There'll be more later."

Jenny folded her arms. "The story's dying."

"We'll see. We'll see."

"You were successful with the coat, certainly, but it's not important any more."

"We'll see, dear," Jason said with emphasis. He put the newspaper aside and bent to his work.

Jenny went into the kitchen.

Presently, coming to the reluctant conclusion that the shoes were finished, Jason set them aside and got out a pile of magazines. From these he started to cut photographs—faces, places, scenes from films. He told himself he would need them sometime, as planned all along, but not necessarily tomorrow.

At ten o'clock they switched on the television. They learned of a train crash in Russia, the Queen's cold, an election in Ottawa, the death of an opera singer, a strike . . .

Jason grew more despondent with every passing second, with every fall from expectancy when, one item finished, the reader began another of a similar unwanted type. At last came:

"The Vanetti case. In an Oxford Street department store this morning, a raincoat was found. It was the colour and make worn by the missing actress. Police searched the store and surrounding streets, with no result. Miss Vanetti's husband, the actor Hull Rainer, was unable to identify the coat positively. Now let's hear from the weather man."

Jenny switched off the set. She turned to look at Jason quizzically. He said a dull, "Yes, it was a flop."

"The day after tomorrow?"

"Yes."

"Morning or afternoon, Jason? Morning would be best."

"All right," he said irritably. "The morning." He got up and went into the bathroom.

While the tub was filling, he cleaned his teeth and undressed. Soaking, he thought about Jenny's latest personality change. The obvious angles covered, it occurred to him that it might be due to neglect. Her abruptness could be saying, "If you don't want me, I don't want you." It was true that he had been inattentive lately. Jason next realised, with surprise, that he and Jenny had not made love for some time; not, in fact, since Elsie had been in the house.

Feeling uncomfortable, Jason excused himself.

It wouldn't have been right, he thought with frail logic, doing that sort of thing while the poor girl was lying in the next room alone and comfortless. It just wouldn't have been right.

• • • • • •

Jason started work at seven the following morning. He continued during and after the breakfast he made for Elsie and himself. Not permitting the lounging which had become a habit, he sat beside Elsie and held her hand, sometimes both hands, while urging from her the remoter recollections and secondary personalities of her life. His manner was firm. He drew Elsie back to the mainstream whenever she was inclined to roam.

Only once during the morning did he soften. This was when Elsie, talking of her days in repertory, told how the cast had clubbed together to buy her a birthday present. Not being able to agree on the gift, they gave her the money. She bought beer and food, and threw a party for the cast.

Jason smiled. He lifted her hand and kissed it.

Straightening, firm again, he went back to work and temporarily destroyed a happy memory.

At noon he went out onto the landing. Jenny was ironing one of her dresses on a board set up near the kitchen door. She said:

"There was nothing in the papers about the coat. Not a line."

"It doesn't matter. Listen I've got an idea."

"What about?"

"Elsie."

Jenny paused. "Going to put it off for another day?"

"No," Jason said. "That's settled. She goes tomorrow."

"Good."

"That's to do with my idea. The reward. The twenty-five thousand pounds."

"There's no safe way we can get it, Jason."

"No, I know. I didn't mean that. I meant we should try to arrange things so that *someone* gets it. You know? Someone deserving."

Jenny put down the iron. She looked at Jason with a warmth he hadn't seen in her face for days. Softly, she said, "That's a marvellous idea."

"You think so?"

"Yes, Jason. Lovely."

"And sensible?"

"Absolutely."

Clasping his hands behind, he began to pace. "Trouble is, we're liable to pick on somebody shabby who turns out to be a miser worth millions. Or a bum who's deserted his wife and kids. Or a pickpocket. Or someone totally wrong."

"Right," Jenny said. She leaned stiff-armed on the ironing board, her stance keen. "So the answer is, we pick someone we know."

"Oh?"

"Of course. We wouldn't come into it ourselves, not as far as the person's concerned. Too risky. We'd simply fix it so that he or she finds Elsie."

Jason said, "Yes. Good. Very good. That fixing, though."

"We'll worry about it later. First let's settle on a person. Really deserving. Who do we know?"

Jason went to lean against the bannister. He looked at Jenny, she looked at him, they both smiled and said together:

"Angela!"

They went on smiling.

"Oh, Jason, she's perfect."

"Hell, yes."

The girl's husband was in a TB sanitorium in Scotland. Although all treatment was free, and the family's upkeep taken care of by the National Assistance Board, Angela and her three children were living at subsistence level in a wretched two-room apartment.

Jenny said breathlessly, "Just think what it would mean, all that money. They could all be together. Scotland. Or they could go to live in Switzerland or Arizona. My God, Jason."

"It's fabulous, Jen. We've got to do it."

"Oh, we must, we must."

Jason nodded deeply, his eyes on the floor. "So now we think method. Part of that is getting Angela out and about somewhere. We can't drop Elsie on her doorstep."

"I could ask her to meet me," Jenny said, then shook her head. "No, we've got to stay out of it completely. She'd be bound to talk of how she came to be in that particular place."

Jason said, "Tell you what, you could ring her up for a chat. Just to say hi. Tell her you're calling from Devonshire. Ask what she's been doing with herself and what she's about to do. See?"

"Yes. Great. She might be going out tomorrow."

"Or this afternoon, or tonight."

"You could have Elsie ready by then?"

"I'd try. Go and phone. I'll make the sandwiches."

Jenny left quickly.

Jason went into the kitchen. Pleased and stimulated, he began slicing bread. He whistled. He wondered why he had not thought of this idea before. He wondered why he had thought of it now.

Before Jason had finished the sandwiches, Jenny was back. Her eyes had sparkle. She was like the Jenny of old. Putting a hand on Jason's arm, she said:

"Tomorrow morning. That's a good sign. It's what you wanted. I'm so thrilled."

"Where's she going?"

"Covent Garden. Very early. Eight o'clock. She goes a couple of times a week. A dealer she knows there, he lets her have fruit and vegetables at wholesale prices."

"Yes, she told us once. She walks. It's not far from where she lives."

"I know. I'd forgotten."

Though happy at this moment, Jason made his face suitably solemn. "Right," he said. "That's it. Covent Garden. Tonight I'll go to scout out the area and think up a plan."

Jenny smiled at him. "This is beautiful, Jason. Beautiful."

"Oh, it's all right."

"Move away," she said, giving him a gentle shove. "You make terrible sandwiches."

After lunch, Jason went back to work. He had with him his notes and the pictures scissored from magazines. He alternated questions with the showing of photographs: "Do you remember a man named . . . ?" "Does this face mean anything to you?"

In the main, Elsie's answers were negative. Occasionally she would say, "There's something familiar there." Which was good enough for Jason. Never did Elsie say, "Yes."

The session lasted all afternoon and evening. It went to Jason's satisfaction save for one point. This troubled him at first. Finally he concluded that the danger it represented was slight, since everything else connected with the play had been eradicated. Only the theme remained, a mere abstraction, the one which, when asked what a picture of a house at night meant to her, caused Elsie to frown and say, "Something evil."

At last the work ended. Jason stood up, stretched, took a turn around the room. He looked at the walls, the floor, the furnishings. He knew every detail, felt as if he had spent six months here instead of less than a sporadic fortnight. And that feeling bred no contempt. He had liked being here. It was curious, Jason thought, how one could become fond of a place so bare and mundane.

He stood behind the one chair. Grave, he looked down at the untidy crown of Elsie's head. Tomorrow, he thought. He rested his hands gently on her shoulders.

12

It was dusk. Lights stationary and moving made baby dazzles. They gave prettiness to the gaunt street along which Hull Rainer was driving.

He had turned his open sports car off the main artery in order to be out of the evening rush, to be able to dawdle, to enjoy his happiness.

On the passenger seat, folded, lay a raincoat. Hull had just collected it from the police station, where he had been obliged to pretend interested in the lab report:

Enough dust had been gathered from the seams to match with that of a location—should said location be found. Minute stains on the lapels were caused by (A) green pea soup of Heinz; (B) porridge; (C) cocoa, brand unestablished. The pockets were empty and clean. Lint on the hem was a 40–60 mixture of wool and rayon, and possibly came from a blanket.

Hull had asked, "No bloodstains?"

Chief Inspector Wilkinson, face as Sphinx-like as ever, had shaken his head. "Nothing at all of, shall we say, a sinister nature."

"And you've still no idea how it got in the store?"

"None whatever."

Hull had made a nice job of running a hand back and forth across his brow. Olivier would not have bettered it, nor the sighed, "When is it all going to end, I wonder."

Changing gear, Hull smiled. It amused him to think that he had once been scared of the detective. Now, stone-face Wilkinson was in his pocket. Had been ever since he had given his alibi with, "The reason I've been holding back, Inspector, was to protect the girl's reputation, innocent though the evening was."

The alibi had been checked, of course, and Nan had played her part. Everything was ducky, except for Nan Mountford herself, who was becoming a nuisance with her telephone calls. She would have to be given the firm brush.

Hull brought the car to a stop by a pedestrian crossing. Two girls stood on the kerb. As they moved forward, they looked at the driver with nods of thanks, looked again with recognition, nudged one another.

Hull felt super. He winked and drove on. This, he told himself, is the life.

Hull's happiness stemmed from an event yesterday and from another still to come. The first, in his agent's office, had been the news that:

"Baby, ITV want you for a series."

"Hey," Hull said, spreading his arms, "You got me a job."

"A job? You're kidding. I've had four TV men after you. I played 'em like trout. I was holding out for a big one, and this is it. A fourteen-part series."

"I love you, George."

"And you'll love the role. Meaty. Private eye with heart of gold. Can you do it?"

"Can birds fly?"

The event still to come, that was an hour away: a party at the home of Samuel Finegold, the motion-picture producer.

Hull couldn't believe that he had been invited simply to be told he was not wanted for a part in *The Road Turns Back*. On the other hand, he thought, Finegold had a reputation as a man with a cruel sense of humour. But that could be sour grapes, a brickbat from the losers. One of whom Hull Rainer was not. Like George Case had said, "You're hot, baby."

Although not confident, Hull was excited. So much so that he felt disinclined to spend the intervening hour at home, or in a bar, or to be in any way static. He needed to be moving. It matched his mood and his career.

He continued driving slowly along quiet streets. From time to time he spurted from twenty to sixty, just to feel that surge, and then feel the tension of braking.

He was already in the area where the movie mogul lived. He had been by the place once—a detached Georgian residence in stucco painted an immaculate white.

Passing the house again, Hull mused that there was where he might stop being Mr Vanetti.

Which reminded him of his wife's disappearance, the Vanetti Affair. He thought of all the comings and goings, the reporters, police, the cranks. He had come through it very well indeed. And bad turned to good. The only real disappointment had been over the raincoat. Telling the press it may not be Elsie's had failed to add the newsworthy bit of mystery he had hoped for. But still. The case lived. Meanwhile there would be Part Two of the heart-warming and Rainer-boosting "My Life With Elsie."

Content, Hull lit a cigarette and went on idling.

When at length he presented himself at Finegold's house, Hull was taken by a servant to an upstairs room. It had twenty-five or thirty people, a sedate crowd. Voices and music tapes were low.

In the overlapping but decidedly separate worlds of "acting" and "showbiz," this was more like the parties he went to with Elsie; and which normally bored him; he preferred the gulp-gorge-grope type.

The host came to greet Hull. He wore a professional smile. "Mr Rainer. How nice."

"Thank you for asking me, Mr Finegold."

"You liked the script, I understand."

"Brilliant."

"It needs work," the producer said. From a passing tray he took a glass of champagne and handed it to Hull, who said:

"Yes, of course, but you can see the potential."

"Quite."

"The part of the younger man, it's very good."

Samuel Finegold nodded absently. He was looking around the room. "There she is," he said. "Come along, Mr Rainer. I want you to meet someone."

After sipping to lower the champagne level, Hull followed through the crowd. He exchanged smiles with familiar faces. The next face he saw was so familiar that he felt his scalp prickle.

Simone Lavilla. The host was waiting for him beside Simone Lavilla.

Tall, beautiful, enigmatic, the Franco-Hispanic actress had been a star for almost twenty years, and was still not yet forty. As a teenager, Hull had worshipped her from the cheap seats. As a man, he had respected her charisma and drawing power from a low but knowledgeable rung on the professional ladder. Simone Lavilla was in the grand tradition of movie queens. She was a terrible actress, but only had to gaze into the lens to make hearts beat faster.

Hull's heart was tapping now. After an introduction, the host had left. Hull and Simone Lavilla were standing close and talking. The star's magnetism and sexuality were so strong that Hull knew nothing of the conversation other than that it had to do with Madrid.

He was stunned by Simone's presence, her large, dark eyes and her husky voice; and with the growing idea, the joyous idea, that the actress found him attractive.

A woman came and drew Simone away. She looked back with a smile which, it seemed to Hull, held promise.

He was sweating. He patted a handkerchief on his brow and top lip. He quickly drained his glass.

Comparatively settled, Hull looked about for the drinks. A bar was set up in a corner. He went over. A white-jacketed barman poured him a whisky and soda. He drained it.

At a tap on his arm, Hull turned. Samuel Finegold, his smile nearer nature, said, "She likes you."

"What?"

"Simone. She thinks you'll be fine in the part."

Unable to speak, Hull nodded.

The producer asked, "Could you be ready for exteriors September tenth?"

Hull nodded again.

"Good. I'll talk terms with George Case tomorrow." He moved away on, "Enjoy yourself."

Hull handed his glass to the barman and indicated a refill. He closed his eyes. He thought: Elsie baby, wherever you are, please stay away a little longer.

PART THREE

13

Once, when Jason Galt was a child, his family had moved to another house. On the last day, waiting for the furniture van, Jason had felt a sadness in the old home, as if it had owned a soul.

It was like that now in the Shank Place flat; like a dying. Nor did the gloom of early morning give any help. The three people sitting on the curiously appointed landing were silent, still, somber.

Jason, arms folded, gazed at the floor. He wore his shabby overcoat and flat cap. Jenny sat on the couch, hunched forward. She was in her usual jeans and sweater.

Elsie sat opposite Jason at the table. She stared sleepily at the wall. Her dress was crumpled, her shoes were decrepit-looking, her hair was a collection of tangles. Dirt lay in the creases of her hands; the fingernails were black. More dirt lay on her face, heightening the lines and making her appear older. She was pale from lack of daylight.

Jason glanced up at her from time to time, then at the clock on the breakfront, then back at the floor.

The clock ticked, Jenny cleared her throat, there were distant traffic noises.

Again Jason looked at the clock. It showed seven-fifteen. He confirmed this with his watch and said, "All right."

Jenny twitched at the abrupt sound of his voice. She smiled and got up. From the table she lifted a cloche hat. She put it on Elsie, carefully tucking in all the hair.

Jason had not moved. He said, "Stand up, Elsie." The actress got to her feet.

Jenny went into the front bedroom. She returned with a pillow and an overcoat. The former, fat, had a loop of ribbon stitched to one end. The coat was a bulky mud-coloured tweed which fastened with three large buttons.

Jenny put the ribbon over Elsie's head. The pillow lay on her stomach between breasts and groin. Next, Jenny helped Elsie into the overcoat and did up the buttons.

Jason nodded, satisfied. As during the dress rehearsal the night before, on his returned from Covent Garden, the actress looked the part of a pregnant woman to a faultless degree: the bulk, her paleness, the flat shoes, her lethargic movements.

Jason got up. "Let's go."

They all went downstairs and outside, Jenny and Elsie arm in arm, Jason walking a little way ahead.

Shank Place was quiet and grey. Over the road, a woman in robe and hair-rollers appeared briefly to take in milk bottles. She didn't look across the street.

The trio reached the corner, went on. Jason lengthened his stride until he had formed between himself and the women a ten-yard gap, which he then maintained.

Apart from a bakery and a newsagent, the shops were closed. Traffic was light. There were few people about.

Jason led the way for fifteen minutes. At a junction he stopped to wait for the women. When they joined him he said quietly, "So far so good."

"Yes," Jenny said. "Let's hope for a cab."

"There'll be plenty."

Jason was right. There were ample vacant taxies heading for duty in Central London. He flagged one down. They got in and shared the seat. Jason said, "Long Acre, please."

He looked out of the window as the cab moved off, looking at the bleak morning scene. He wondered why he felt no pleasurable excitement. The scheme he had planned, the one which at first had seemed impossible, was three-quarters of the way to fruition. And he felt nothing. Nerves, he thought. The stimulation would come later.

He looked at the woman beside him. Her eyes were dreamily on a folding seat. Jason looked at Jenny. She gave him an unsteady smile.

He asked, keeping his voice low, "Worried?"

"Only a little. I'll be okay."

"Good girl."

The time was twenty minutes to eight when the driver, as directed, stopped at the corner of Long Acre and Neat Street. They got out. Jenny took Elsie aside while Jason paid. He added a normal, unmemorable tip.

He was glad the journey had turned out quietly well. He had not liked the idea of a taxi, but had been forced to agree with Jenny that it would be safer than the underground—one man's notice against that of dozens.

Jason joined the women. They went across the road.

Two minutes later the morning torpor had gone. It was as if time had taken a three-hour jump ahead. Covent Garden was a minor bedlam.

The open-fronted fruit and vegetable warehouses were blazing with light and choked with bustling men. The roadway was crammed with trucks, some delivering, some collecting. There were shouts, horn-blasts, arguments between drivers, calls for clearance from porters pushing trollies. Exhaust fumes fought to dominate the sickly stench of new and rotting fruit.

"And this has been going on since dawn," Jenny said, momentarily lifted from concern.

"Over here," Jason said. "Follow me."

He led through the trucks, past trollies and around a group of heavy-eyed American tourists with a chanting guide. There was too much going on for anyone to pay Jason and the women any attention.

They went on to a quieter stretch, passed between two vehicles to the kerb, rounded a vast pile of orange boxes and went through a brick archway.

It was the entrance to a mission hall. Ten feet in, it ended against a gate-covered door. The walls had posters that said you should come to Jesus.

Jenny took Elsie to the gate. Jason stayed near the arch.

He had a clear view of the opposite pavement right along to the corner, a distance of a hundred yards. This, Jenny had said she felt sure, was the way Angela Prentice would come.

A man appeared in front of the arch. He stopped. Slovenly, middle-aged, unshaven, he stood staring at Jason with swimming eyes. He swayed. He seemed to be drunk.

"It's closed," Jason said.

"Huh?"

Hating himself and hating the man, Jason said, "Move on. It's closed."

A shaky hand came out in accompaniment to the litany, "Not a bite in two days."

Jason quickly produced a coin and slapped it into the hand. The man nodded and walked on. Jason leaned out to watch. Jenny's voice at his elbow asked:

"What was that?"

"Meths drinker. The area's full of 'em."

"Poor bastard."

Jason hated himself still more. Which he forgot on turning and seeing Jenny. He was startled at the changed appearance, even though it was expected.

Jenny had now become the pregnant woman. She wore the pillow and the coat. Settling the cloche hat in place, she asked, "All right?"

"Yes, perfect."

"Listen. What if Angela should see us."

"She won't," Jason said. "Don't worry about it. Keep your eye on the corner."

"Right."

Jason passed her and went to the back of the chill, damp passage. Elsie stood facing the gate. Moving close, Jason put his hands on her upper arms. He began to speak in a low, firm voice.

"Elsie. In a minute I am going to show you a woman. I will point her out to you. At a signal from me you will come awake and go to that woman. You will cross the street, go to her and say, 'Can you help me, please. I seem to be lost.' Do you understand?"

"Yes."

"What will you say?"

"Can you help me, please. I seem to be lost."

Jason said, "She, and others later on, will ask you who you are, where you've been, what your name is. You will not be able to tell them because you do not know. You will say, 'It's silly, but I can't remember anything.' Try it."

"It's silly," Elsie said in her distant voice, "but I can't remember anything."

From the arch came a hissed, "She's here!"

Jason left Elsie, moved quickly to the front. He said, "She's ahead of time. I'll need a few more minutes."

"Wait till she's done her shopping."

"Of course."

They were both watching carefully the girl across the street. Angela Prentice was tall and thin and plain. She wore an ankle-length dress under a cardigan. Her fair hair was in a ponytail. She looked tired.

"Poor Angela," Jenny said.

Jason said, "Rich Angela."

The girl was pushing a pram. Cumbersome and old-fashioned, it held two children, one a baby and the other a toddler. Behind walked a boy of about four. Straddle-legged, he was using a broken umbrella as a hobbyhorse.

Defensively, Jenny said, "She keeps them clean."

Angela Prentice drew level, went on and passed from view beyond a truck. "Call me as soon as she comes back," Jason said. He returned to Elsie.

She was shivering now without the coat. Holding her again by the upper arms, Jason asked:

"What will you say to people when they want to know about you?"

"It's silly, but I can't remember anything."

"Correct. They will press you, keep on with their questions. You will say you have the impression you have been walking around for days. Just wandering. Everything is a blur. Before that, you remember nothing. Is that understood?"

Elsie said, "Yes."

"There is one last thing I want you to forget. It is a name. Elsie Vanetti. From this moment on, that name is not known to you. Clear?"

"Yes."

"Fine. Good girl. In a minute, when I have shown you the woman, I will give you the signal. This will be it. Listen." He snapped his fingers close to her ear. "All right?"

"Yes."

"You will then walk across the street to the woman. You will not look back. You will not have any desire to look back. You will be perplexed. You will feel strange, unsure of yourself. You will know, however, that the woman will help you. No one else can."

Jason dropped his hands and stepped back. He had done all he could. Once Elsie left the arch, it was no longer in his power.

He glanced behind, asking, "Anything?"

"Not yet," Jenny said. "She might have to wait to be served."

"She wouldn't go the other way?"

"I doubt it."

Jason turned back to Elsie. Her shivering was stronger now. Jason wondered if he should open his coat and bring her inside it, close to him. Give her some warmth. Close to him. The poor girl might catch cold. She'd had enough to put up with lately. It was about time she had a little comfort. Warmth. Close to him.

Jenny said gaspingly, "Jason, Jason she's here!"

He felt a thud under his heart. Turning Elsie around, he drew her to the front of the passage.

Across the street, Angela Prentice was walking level. On the pram between the two children were piles of paper bags and a small wooden box.

"There," Jason said, his voice hard. "See that woman with a pram?"

"Yes."

"She will help you. Listen, here's the signal." He brought his hand close to her ear and snapped his fingers. He and Jenny moved back. They watched Elsie from behind.

A ripple of movement passed over her body. She took a deep breath. She made a murmur, like a sleeper awakening. She looked around, she looked down at herself, she looked across the street.

She moved forward.

Jason, who had stopped the action of his lungs, started to breathe again. Jenny gripped his arm tightly.

Elsie left the arch, crossed the sidewalk and set off over the road.

Jenny gasped suddenly. Jason went rigid.

A truck was coming.

Elsie had almost reached the middle of the road. She was looking neither right nor left. Now she jerked her head around at a screech of brakes; saw the truck; ran.

Jenny said, "God." Jason felt sweat prickling his armpits. He let his tense body droop.

The truck had passed by. Elsie, standing on the far kerb, was watching it go. She seemed bewildered. One hand reached up to fiddle with a strand of hair.

Angela Prentice was midway to the corner.

"Hurry," Jenny whispered. "*Hurry.*"

Elsie stared along the street after the girl with the pram. Dropping her hand she started to walk, moving quickly. She broke into a hesitant semi-run.

Jason was not aware of wincing at the pain of Jenny's grip on his arm. He felt as a dimension within himself the distance between the archway and the hurrying woman.

Elsie reached the pram. She brought Angela to a stop with a gesture. She spoke. Angela's expression, which had been one of surprise, slowly turned to resignation.

She shook her head. She walked on.

Elsie stood alone.

"Christ," Jenny said. "She thinks Elsie's a down-and-outer."

Angela came to a slow halt. Leaving the pram she turned and walked back. She brought out a purse, opened it, peered inside.

She looked up on stopping beside Elsie, who was speaking again. Angela blinked, frowned. She stared closely at the face of the actress. Next, her mouth sagging open, she eased back.

In a whispered shriek, Jenny said, "That's it! She's tumbled!"

Angela spoke. Elsie answered. The following moment they were walking off together.

Angela pushed the pram with one hand while holding Elsie's arm with the other and glancing repeatedly at her face. The boy rode his umbrella horse behind.

The moving tableau turned the corner and went from sight. The couple in the arch looked at one another. Jenny smiled tremulously. Jason nodded.

●●●●●●

Their home district was awake and active when they came from the Underground station. Shops were busy, schoolchildren bustled, road traffic was dense. The climbing sun created glints and flashes which increased the impression of vivacity.

"What a beautiful morning," Jenny said, lifting back her head and running a hand through her hair.

She had removed the hat and unbuttoned her coat. The pillow Jason carried under his arm. He had pushed the flock down at one end and wrapped the slack material with the ribbon. They looked like any other couple on their way to the laundromat.

"Let's go on walking a while," Jenny said. "I don't want to go back just yet."

Jason's answer was immediate. "Neither do I."

"It'll be lovely in the park this morning."

"We'll go there."

They walked on in silence. During their removal from Covent Garden, the wait on the Underground platform and the train ride, they had exhausted the subject of Angela Prentice and the reward.

Now they could only cover worn ground. There had been no attempt to talk of the future in respect of Elsie.

Jenny's look of satisfaction was beginning to fade. It was as if, one task accomplished, she were turning reluctantly to the next.

Jason's face showed nothing. It was a fair mirror for his emotions. He felt empty. This, he assured himself, was the natural let-down after all the pressures and excitements. It was only to be expected that he should miss, in a sense, the tension of the past days. Which was good. He could build up reserves for the assault to come.

In the park they moved off the asphalt paths. The damp grass smelled sweet. A delight of birdsong came from the trees. The greenness was as restful as a lullaby.

Jason went on feeling empty, neither seeing nor hearing. The expression on Jenny's face had become one of apprehension. They were still silent.

At length Jenny said, "Let's sit over there."

They went to the bench and sat. Leaning forward, forearms on knees, Jason stared away over the green.

Jenny cleared her throat. She said, "Jason?"

"Yes?"

It was unexpected, what she said next. Even startling. Yet Jason didn't look around or change position. Nor was his emptiness greatly affected. He merely recorded the matter of:

"I'm leaving you."

Silence again.

Jenny asked, "Did you hear me, Jason?" There was strain in her voice.

He said, "Yes."

"I'm leaving you."

Jason turned his head to the side, toward Jenny, but didn't look at her. "All right, Jen," he said gently. "If that's what you want."

"I think it's best, dear. I really do." She was speaking easier now. "I've thought it over carefully."

"Is it the affair?"

"Affair?"

"Elsie. The abduction."

"Well, yes, partly," Jenny said. "I know I can't talk you out of going ahead with the plan. And I'm afraid. I have the feeling it's not going to turn out quite the way you hope. Call it intuition."

"You want to be free of it."

"Yes. I'm guilt-ridden about that, though. Rats and sinking ships."

Jason sat up and turned to her. She had a firm smile. He wondered if she were crying.

He said, "Please don't feel guilty. You've been marvellous. I couldn't have got this far without you. It's not desertion. Your share of the work is over."

"Yes."

"But I think you're wrong about how it's going to turn out."

"I hope so," Jenny said. "I really do."

"Even if it doesn't go right for me, it can't go much against me."

"Well, as I said, that's only part of it." She touched his arm lightly. "Our time's over. It's been great, but it was only a temporary thing. We both knew that, even though we never said it."

Jason nodded. "Yes, Jen."

"We have no future together. It's best we break away now before we become a habit. That happens, and it's dreary."

"You're right, I suppose," Jason said. "But I'm going to miss you. You're a sweet girl, a fine person."

Jenny lowered her eyes and eased back, smiling, smiling. "Don't, Jason."

He looked away. After a moment he asked, "When did you think of going?"

"Now. Today."

"Oh."

"I'd planned it for the day Elsie went. I've fixed up to go and stay with someone."

"Who?"

"I don't want you to know," Jenny said. "A girl I shared a flat with years ago. If you knew where I was, you might try to make contact. I want a clean break."

Jason turned to her again. "Jen, if everything works out right, naturally I'll want to make contact. You helped in this, you deserve part of the proceeds. In fact, I'm determined that you'll benefit."

She shrugged. "I don't know. I don't know if I want to be paid for being involved in this thing."

"Don't think of it as payment."

"Well. Whatever."

"Jenny, promise that if all goes well you'll get in touch with me. I'll feel awful if I can't at least make you an offer."

"All right, then. I promise."

"Thanks."

Jenny got up. About to do the same, Jason eased back onto the bench again when Jenny said:

"No. Please. You stay here."

"I could help you."

"I've been ready for days. I've washed and ironed my things, cleared out stuff I don't want. Everything's ready for putting in my suitcase."

"I see."

"I'll be out of the house in fifteen minutes," she said. The strain had returned to her voice. She was smiling broadly.

Jason said, and felt the inadequacy of, "You've been great."

"You have as well. I don't regret one minute of it. I'll always think well of you." She turned away with a fierce smile, circled the bench and walked off.

Jason stared into the distance.

14

Hull Rainer had imagined, on those occasions when he spared it a thought, that the end of the Vanetti Affair would be signalled by a ring at the apartment door. Elsie, keyless, would be back looking sheepish or defiant; a reporter would tell of tracking her down to a remote hotel; a policeman would say, "Prepare yourself for bad news, sir."

But it was the telephone. It rang when Hull was finishing his breakfast of toast and coffee. He sauntered through to the living room.

The voice, male, said, "This is Bow Lane Police Station, Mr Rainer. We have a lady here who answers the description of your wife."

"And what does the lady herself answer?"

"Beg pardon?"

"She must have told you who she is."

"She doesn't know, sir. She seems to have lost her memory."

"Clothing, then."

"The shoes are the make we have listed. In fact, sir, we're sure this is Miss Vanetti. We'd like you to come along and make a positive identification."

Driving away from Lancaster Gate ten minutes later, Hull had stopped thinking of the woman at Bow Lane. He felt somehow she could not be Elsie. It would turn out to be yet another false alarm.

Hull was dwelling on his plans for the day re Simone Lavilla. Getting hold of her ex-directory telephone number would be the first hurdle. Then he would call her to say how happy he was to be making a movie with a star of her standing, to ask how she herself saw the part he was to play, and to wonder aloud if they should get together for a discussion of the scenes they were going to share.

It would run on from there, Hull thought.

He hummed cheerily throughout the crawl in the West End

traffic and the search near his destination for a parking slot. He finally left the car two streets from the police station. He stopped whistling only on entering the grim building.

It was quiet in the front office. A lone constable commanded the desk, another sat staring at a typewriter. On a bench-seat was a woman with three children. She looked at Hull intently. Her eyes were red. She seemed to be trembling.

If that's the one, Hull thought, bored and relieved.

The desk constable asked, "Mr Rainer?"

"Yes."

"Down the passage, sir. Second door."

Hull went on, wrinkling his nose at the smell of disinfectant. He tapped on the second door, entered—and came to a shaken halt.

Elsie was there. His wife. Elsie.

Bedraggled, forlorn, she sat at a table with a policewoman. They both got up. Elsie looked at Hull timidly.

He, surprised and nonplussed, forced the semblance of a smile, also a delighted-sounding, "Darling!"

The policewoman asked happily, "She's your wife?"

"Of course, of course," Hull said. "Elsie angel." He went toward her, his arms out. He stopped awkwardly and his smile became foolish: Elsie had drawn back.

He asked, "Darling, what is it?"

The policewoman said, "She's lost her memory, sir. We've sent for a doctor."

"Elsie. It's me. Hull. I'm your husband."

She was staring at him. She murmured, "Husband."

"Yes, love. You mean you don't know me?"

She shook her head slowly. She appeared to be close to tears. "I'm sorry. I'm very sorry."

"Darling, don't worry about it. We'll have you better again in no time."

The door opened. From then on, all was confusion.

In came Chief Inspector Wilkinson and his aide Bart, another two detectives, a doctor and two ambulance men. Hull and everyone else talked, asked, milled around.

A detective took Hull out to the front office and introduced him to a Mrs Prentice, who, apparently, had found Elsie in nearby Covent Garden. A group of reporters barged in. Flashbulbs popped, questions were shouted, a police sergeant told the men that if they didn't keep it quiet he would throw them out. Hull felt dazed and low.

The doctor came and drew him to one side. He said he would like to take Elsie to the hospital. She looked all right, but he would like to run a series of tests.

"What for?"

"General health, and to see if there's been brain damage. The fugue, you know."

"Fugue?"

"Loss of memory. If you prefer your own doctor, of course, that will be perfectly all right."

Hull shook his head.

There was another flurry of questions and flashbulbs as Elsie was led through the front office. Outside, a small crowd had gathered. Some people clapped.

Hull, Elsie and the doctor sat together in the back of the ambulance. Elsie looked distraught. Her hands fidgeted. Of Hull she asked:

"What's your name, please?"

"Hull Rainer."

She wrinkled her brow. "But I've just been told my name's Vanetti."

"It is. You kept it for the stage. Your married name is Rainer."

"I'm an actress. How strange. It's like a dream. Maybe it *is* one."

The doctor said, "You'll be all right soon."

Hull noticed him properly for the first time. Young and dressed sloppily, he had a long nose and keen eyes.

Elsie asked, "If I've lost my memory, how do I know what an actress is? How do I know this is an ambulance? How do I know the names for things—hand, dress, street?"

"Partial amnesia," the doctor said, patting her shoulder. "It's the most common kind. The other, total, is where a person becomes a speechless infant again."

"Thank God for small mercies."

Hull told her, "You always say that."

She looked at him blankly. "How strange."

"Everything's going to be fine," the doctor said. "First a nice hot bath, then we'll pop you into bed. I'll try and wangle a private room."

"But that would mean I'm somebody special," Elsie said. She smiled faintly. "You see? I know about the National Health Service. Free medical treatment for all."

"Quite normal, Miss Vanetti."

"And you *are* somebody special," Hull said. "You're famous."

Disbelievingly: "I'm not."

The doctor said, "I've seen all your films, and I've seen you in the play you're in now. It's called *Maybe Tomorrow*. Does that mean anything to you?"

"No."

Hull told her, "You disappeared two weeks ago. I've been going frantic."

She shook her head slowly, unhappily.

The ambulance stopped. They got out and went into a vast, stone-floored lobby. It was echoing with voices and clattering footsteps. There seemed to be dozens of white-dressed people present.

"I phoned we were coming," the doctor said. "Obviously the word has spread. It's not every day we get a celebrity."

Openly or covertly, everyone was staring. Hull got a fair share. Yet he was relieved to be shown into an antechamber, was glad to be alone.

Lighting a cigarette he paced around the centre table. He was still dazed. Elsie had been missing for months, it felt like, and now suddenly she was back. Or part of her was. She seemed to be not Elsie at all, but an imposter. It was eerie, too, the way she looked at him without recognition.

He was on his second cigarette when the door opened. Detective Sergeant Bart said, "The Inspector's going to check Miss Vanetti's clothes, sir. Would you care to be present?"

Hull shrugged an indifferent affirmative.

Wilkinson was waiting in an upper room. It was all white, including the furniture. Thinking of morgues, Hull shuddered. He and the two detectives stood looking at each other.

Chief Inspector Wilkinson said, "Well, congratulations. Your wife's back safely."

Hull squared his shoulders. "Yes, it's all over."

"Well, I wouldn't say that, Mr Rainer. We've still got to find out what's been happening."

"I've talked with Mrs Prentice, but she can't tell us much. I've got a team of men in Covent Garden now. They may come up with something. She can't have appeared there out of thin air."

"I hope," Hull said caustically, "you haven't been wasting too much time trying to prove I murdered Elsie."

Wilkinson ignored that. His face didn't even betray the fact that he had heard. He said:

"The doctor's going to let us talk to Miss Vanetti in a while. She may give us something to go on."

"She's back," Hull said. "That's all that matters."

"To you, perhaps. Not to us—if there's been a criminal act."

Hull was about to tell the policeman that he seemed disappointed Elsie wasn't dead, that her safe return must be a blow to his case of international interest. Hull stopped himself. That interest, he thought, that lovely free publicity. A criminal act would keep it alive.

"Yes," he said. "Something odd could very well have been going on. I'll give you all the help I can, Inspector."

"Thank you, sir."

An orderly came in. He left after putting a basket on the white metal table. There was silence as Wilkinson emptied the basket of its contents and carefully examined each garment.

At length Hull said, "Everything's filthy."

"Mm. Looks as if she hasn't been undressed for some time. What condition were these shoes in?"

"Good shape. They're fairly new."

"*Were.* Awful mess now."

Hull asked, "Can you tell anything from all this?"

"No. Maybe the lab can."

The three men were still looking at the soiled clothes when the doctor came in, briskly and rubbing his hands together.

"Five minutes," he said. "I don't want you to keep her longer than that. And be quiet about it, please. She could be in a mild state of shock. It would be better, in fact, if you came back tomorrow."

Wilkinson said, "It's important, Doctor, that we talk to her as close to the event as possible."

"Five minutes, then. Come along."

Hull, walking a corridor beside the doctor, with Wilkinson at the other side and Bart trailing, asked, "What's this fugue thing all about?"

"To me, a physician, it means tissue damage. We'll be looking particularly for a head wound. Possibly something microscopic. Also, the memory bank of the brain could have been hit by a blood clot, or been stopped in some way from getting nourishment. Or it could be the nervous system. It could even be a brain tumor, but that's not likely, not with the suddenness. As I said, we'll be running lots of tests."

"And if they're negative?"

"Then it's the turn of the psychiatrists."

Wilkinson asked, "Could she have been doped?"

"Well, it's a thought."

"Perhaps you could check—saliva, blood, urine. And watch for needle marks."

"I'll do that, Inspector."

"Could you do an internal as well? Semen, signs of sexual activity?"

Hull shot the policeman a look of disgust, but the doctor said he would talk to the house gynecologist.

"And look for marks of restraint, please. Ankles and wrists."

"I already did, Inspector. There's nothing."

Elsie had a room to herself. She was sitting in bed drinking tea. Her hair, damp, was bunched up on top of her head. To Hull she appeared more of an imposter than ever.

The attendant nurse and the doctor stayed, hovering in the background. The three other men stood by the bed. After pleasantries, Chief Inspector Wilkinson said:

"Could you tell me, please, what's the first thing you remember?"

Elsie lay a hooked forefinger thoughtfully under her bottom lip. It was a gesture Hull knew well.

She said, "Noise and a sweet smell. The place is Covent Garden, I know that. I was looking across the street at a woman with a pram. I had the feeling that she could help me. I went across. And that's all."

"Before that a blank?"

"Yes. It's silly, but I can't remember anything."

Hull said, "You must remember *something*, dear."

She gave him that timid look, shaking her head. "I can't."

"Try. Think. Where did you sleep?"

"I don't know."

"Do you remember being in a cafeteria?"

"No."

Wilkinson asked, "Is there nothing you recall, Miss Vanetti? Even an impression would help. Don't worry if it sounds foolish, sounds something like a dream."

The forefinger went back under her lip. "Well, yes," she said. "I do have this impression. It's of walking. Wandering. Everything is a blur. That's all. There's really nothing else."

The doctor said, "All right, gentlemen."

● ● ● ● ● ●

By noon, Hull had lost his sense of bewilderment. No longer was he unsure of his feelings in regard to the return of his wife. He was pleased.

It could not, he felt, have been better. Nothing sordid was involved, Elsie was still out of his hair at this career-eventful and intrigue-possible time, and the amnesia thing was beautifully newsworthy.

Hull had enjoyed pushing his way with solemn face through the reporters outside the hospital. He had enjoyed telephoning the news to key friends and theatre people. He had enjoyed being called by four TV companies, who asked if they could send trucks to get filmed statements. He had loved calling the *Sunday Standard*, indulging in some mild flirtation with his ghost writer and hearing that the second installment of "My Life With Elsie" would go ahead as planned.

Now he enjoyed having his work done for him by getting a telephone call from Simone Lavilla. She said:

"I have just heard about your wife on the radio. I am happy for you."

Hull made a suitable reply. Discarding his planned approach, he said, "A few friends are coming over tonight to celebrate Elsie's safe return. I'd be honoured if you'd join us."

"That sounds very nice."

"My wife won't be here, of course. She's in hospital."

"Yes," the movie star said again, "that sounds very nice."

At twelve-thirty, Hull changed into clothes which would film well. He went downstairs. The four TV trucks were waiting, as well as a dozen reporters. He made the statement he had worked on carefully. Though solemn, it also had relief and optimism. A crewman asked for his autograph.

Hull walked to a nearby restaurant for a light lunch. Two of the journalists were following him until he told them he had a contract with the *Sunday Standard*. In the restaurant he was a minor sensation. He got a brandy on the house and the chef came out to shake his hand.

Back at the block of flats, all mediamen had gone. Hull went upstairs and into a prolonged session of telephone answering. The news was spreading.

Elsie's mother called from Bristol. She was on her way to London, and why hadn't she been told at once instead of getting it from a neighbour who'd heard it on the radio? Elsie was her own flesh and blood. It was a disgrace that . . .

Nan Mountford had seen it in the early edition of the evening paper. She was so happy for Hull. She would like to see him again as soon as possible. Would he give her a ring when he had a free moment?

The president of the Elsie Vanetti fan club was overjoyed. Loss of memory was nothing, the dear girl would soon be all right again. Did Hull have any objections to the reward being given to Mrs Angela Prentice?

Roger Burn was glad now he hadn't taken the play off. With Elsie back in her part, they could easily have a two-year run on their hands.

The features editor of the *Sunday Standard* would send a man over tomorrow afternoon for an exclusive blow-by-blow story on Elsie's return.

Other calls were from friends and colleagues. Hull himself rang eight people and invited them to a cocktail party at seven. He would have liked to have invited the producer, Samuel Finegold, but didn't want to risk a rejection. Hull's last call was to a delivery-service cafe for canapes.

At five, the official visiting hour, he drove to the hospital. In nearby shops he bought black grapes and two dozen red roses. He posed with these for a press photograph on the steps.

Elsie looked and acted much as before. She still remembered nothing. She had been given a copy of her biography to read; it had no meaning for her; she was unable to relate to any of the people or events.

Being treated as a stranger made Hull uncomfortable. He wanted to leave. Since that would look odd to the staff, he passed time by reading aloud sections of the biography. It was a relief to get away and drive home.

The evening papers had been delivered. Elsie's return was the headline story. There were pictures of her and Hull leaving the police station, one of Hull alone outside his apartment building, one of Covent Garden, one of Mrs Prentice and her three children. Hull was still reading the newspapers when the canapes arrived.

● ● ● ● ● ●

". . . a marriage of convenience."

"I know exactly what you mean, Mr Rainer."

"Hull, please."

"All right, Hull. And you must call me Simone."

The party had been on an hour. Simone Lavilla had been present fifteen minutes. The other guests were film and television people who had been, or could be, useful, plus agent George Case.

Hull had chatted to them all with feigned interest while awaiting the acceptably late arrival of the movie queen. Then had come her entrance to the sound of an unheard trumpet voluntary and her grandiose greeting of everyone. It had been an impressive performance.

Now Hull had Simone to himself. They were standing close in a corner of the room, talking in low voices like thieves. Hull was flattered. He had been so on their first meeting, next on her acceptance of his invitation, now because of their intimacy and the fact that Simone was speaking in her normal English, precise and accentless, rather than the sulky fracturisation beloved by millions.

"A business arrangement," Hull said. "It protects us yet allows us to lead our lives."

"How very sensible. I should have had a similar understanding with my three husbands."

They smiled at each other. Hull sipped his whisky. Simone lifted her glass close to her mouth, and then, looking at Hull, dipped her tongue into the champagne.

Hull said, huskily, "Tomorrow. Lunch. Could we have lunch together? Talk about the film?"

"There are lots of things we could talk about."

"Yes. Sure."

"But, tragically, tomorrow I shall be busy. Preparing. In the evening I fly to Paris for two weeks of dubbing for that last atrocious film I perpetrated."

"Two weeks. That's awful."

"You are young. So am I. Though not as young as you are."

Hull lied, "I'm thirty-five."

Again they exchanged an intimate smile, their heads close. Simone ran finger and thumb languidly up and down the stem of her glass. Hull took a gulp of whisky.

A couple came over to say their thanks and good-byes. Hull noticed only insofar as being annoyed at the interruption. The next to run interference was George Case, but this turned to value when the agent said in his brash way:

"I'm taking a chick out to dinner. Why don't you kids join us?"

Hull looked at Simone. She said, "I love eating."

They drove in the MGB, George Case squeezed complainingly in the token back seat with his date, a screenwriter who shone only in the written word.

The Indian restaurant on Edgeware Road welcomed the foursome like giftless Greeks. Every one of Simone's quibbles was treated with not so much respect as admiration. Hull glowed. And he was glad to be in a group. Being alone with a sex goddess—that would be bad for his concerned-husband image.

Hull had no notion of what food he toyed with. His awareness was given to Simone: her double-entendre jokes, the way she kept his wineglass filled, her hand dropping to his thigh.

They parted from Case and his date outside. Back in the car, Simone said, "Let's go to your place for a nightcap."

Hull drove quickly. He was so stimulated that in addressing a thought to himself in congratulation, he used his real name, something he hadn't done for years.

With drinks before them on the coffee table, Simone and Hull sat on a couch. There was a moment of idle talk. Simone moved close and put her arm around Hull's shoulders. She said softly, "You're cute." He said, "You're fabulous." She asked, "Like to take me to bed?" Hull nodded dumbly.

When he awoke, it was morning. He lay alone on the crumpled bed, smiling in memory of last night's exhausting and thrilling sexual athletics. He semi-hoped Simone had no more action in mind; he wasn't sure if he were capable.

Getting up and putting on a robe, Hull realised Simone had left. On the kitchen table he found a note. It said he was divine, she had taken his phone number, she would call him in a fortnight.

Hull wondered distantly if she had put his number in her stocking. He next wondered, less distantly, if someday she would revile him for being a cheap stud.

He shuddered at the weird thought, laughed nervously and set about making coffee. The telephone rang. The day had begun.

It and the following day were similar to the pattern set yesterday. Hull visited his wife, answered the telephone, talked to his newspaper people. He signed a contract for the TV series. At the hospital he saw his mother-in-law, who was furious at not being recognised by Elsie and refused to be consoled by the same having happened with Hull and friends who had visited. Wilkinson telephoned to say the lab could give nothing interesting on Miss Vanetti's clothes.

On the third day, late afternoon, when Hull left Elsie's room, he found the doctor waiting for him. They strolled along the corridor together. Hull asked about the tests.

"All finished, Mr Rainer. And the news is good. I think."

"You think?"

The doctor smiled. "Your wife is extremely healthy. She has been abused in no way I can discover. Excellent constitution. If, as she believes, she has been wandering around like a homeless soul, it hasn't done her any harm."

"And?"

"So her amnesia must be psychological. Which might be quite a problem. She may need only a mental nudge to bring her memory back, but she may need extended therapy."

"I see."

"Now," the doctor said briskly. "Would you like your wife moved to a psychiatric hospital, or do you want to take her away and use a doctor in private practice?"

Hull said at once, "Hospital. You people seem to know what you're doing."

"Well, there's an excellent place in North London . . ."

Hull got away as soon as he could. The clinical ambience stifled him and put a brake on the euphoria which had obtained with him lately.

Outside, he found a telephone kiosk, dialled Nan Mountford and asked if she were free. She told him to come over.

15

That same evening, as Hull Rainer was driving cheerfully toward Hampstead, Jason Galt was on his way home from the newspaper shop. He read as he walked. The pertinent item concerned the Vanetti Affair. It was short; and on page two.

The actress was still in hospital, still suffering from loss of memory. A hospital spokesman said that so far no cause had been found for her amnesia. A police spokesman said that as yet there was no evidence of foul play.

Jason folded the newspaper and shoved it in the pocket of his windcheater. His handsome face was grave. He felt unmoved by the reported fact that all was going as he wanted and had planned.

Jason was depressed. He had been so for days, since returning from the park to the flat, whose echoing emptiness made him lonely. Disconsolate, he had wandered the silent rooms. He told himself he would soon cheer up.

His depression continued, however. At first, work kept it sporadically in check. He rearranged all the furniture, wiped every smooth surface with a soapy cloth, burned his false beard, cap and old overcoat. Elsie's sunglasses he smashed and took to a lamp-post litterbin two miles away.

Chores finished, there was nothing to do but wait. Wait in dreariness.

Learning via the media that his scheme was prospering gave him no ease. A televised statement by Hull Rainer only made him feel sorry for the anguish he had given the man. Newspaper shots of Elsie—leaving the police station, entering the hospital—created an ache in Jason's chest. He called it loneliness. He thought it surprising how deeply he was missing Jenny.

In his low state, he worried. The end of his scheme caused him hours of fret, like a neurotic who, present perfect, has to content himself with gnawing on future indefinite.

Jason worried about what would be the best approach to Hull

Rainer, about him being unapproachable, or curtly dismissive re the offer of hypnotism help, or, if accepting, about him not wanting the publicity which would be needed. Jason worried about the possibility of doctors curing Elsie's amnesia, about leaving her too long in their hands, about someone else coming up with the idea of hypnotism or recognising such as the cause. He worried about the public losing all interest in the affair if it went on too long and not caring if the actress was cured or not.

He slept badly.

Jason was yawning now as he turned into Shank Place. Nerves, he thought, remembering one of Elsie's reminiscences in which she told of incessant yawns during rep days. Nerves because he always half expected to see a police car standing outside Number Nine.

But there was nothing out of the ordinary. Those cars present were the same old terminals, awaiting the euthanasian hammer of the scrapman. Two children were wrestling with shrieks of laughter. Jason hurried to escape the sound.

Pushing open the door, he saw lying on the inner sill a piece of paper. He picked it up worriedly, relaxed on seeing it was a note from Angela Prentice, started to worry again after reading:

"Hey you two. Are you back from hols yet? Did you see me in the papers? Collected the reward this morning. Call me at once. Urgent. Urgent."

The last two words were underlined.

What could be urgent about it?—Jason wondered. What did she mean? He stared at the twin words until they became ominous, threatening.

Closing the door, he hurried back along the street. One of the children shouted after him an obscene name. Jason found this oddly satisfying.

The nearest public telephone was in a laundromat. Jason got change there, fed the coin slot and dialled. He put a hand over his ear to counter the noise from machines and customers.

When the call signal ended he identified himself.

"Jason!" Angela Prentice screamed. "Darling you! Get my note? Isn't this fantastic? I'm going round the twitch with it all. Harry's back. He's here now. I can't believe any of it."

"Congratulations on the money, Angela."

"Good old formal Jason. I love you madly."

"What's urgent? You said in the note something was urgent."

"Just the party, love. The bash we're throwing to celebrate. It's now. People're arriving. You've got to come, both of you. I'll be mortified if you don't. How's Jenny?"

"As a matter of fact, Jenny and I . . ."

Angela wasn't listening. She bubbled on about the money, her husband's return from the sanitorium, the champagne they'd bought. She ended, "Must fly. More people. Come to the party!"

Leaving the laundromat, Jason moved to the kerb and leaned on a post there. The problem now, he mused, was whether or not to obey Angela's injunction. Would it be worse to go than to stay away? The latter would look strange to the Prentices and others when later he became involved in the Vanetti Affair. In respect of that, either way would look odd, but it could be eased with a hint of intention now.

There were other questions of doubt which arose. Jason got sick of them. Of only one thing he was sure: for the recipient of the reward, he should have chosen a stranger.

He tossed a coin. The party won. He headed for the Underground station.

●●●●●●

The stairs, the hall and the two rooms—one a bedroom—were crowded with laughing people. Bottles of champagne were passing from hand to hand and being poured into beerglasses, cups, tin mugs, soup bowls, jars which had once held baby food. Also making the rounds were plates of thick sandwiches.

Jason, unhappy with the clamour and the joy, accepted the mug of champagne that was thrust into his hand and acted a smile as he made his way through the crush. He intended leaving as soon as he had made his visit known to host and hostess.

Progress was slowed by people he knew. He was forced to pause and exchange boisterous greetings, loud inconsequentials. He felt worse out of shame for feeling so offended, so alien.

Angela was in the bedroom. So were about twenty other people. It took Jason ten minutes and a refill of his mug to get to where Angela was sitting on a bedside table. Her eyes were bright. This was not due to alcohol. As Jason knew, Angela was a non-drinker.

"It's a miracle," she said, after she and Jason had embraced. "I believe in miracles now."

"So do I. I'm very happy for you."

"Seen Harry yet? Where's Jenny? I've left the kids with a neighbour. I'm going to buy them a new outfit apiece tomorrow. We might go to Switzerland, did I tell you that? Have a drink. Have two."

Jason laughed. "It's good to see you so happy."

"Love, I'm over the moon. I've invited everyone I know. If I've forgotten anyone I'll die. But I don't think so. Everyone's here. Even the cops."

Jason stiffened. "The police?"

Angela leaned closer, flicking a direction with her eyes. "That type by the door. He put me through the hoop, so I invited him too for the hell of it."

Jason looked around. He saw an obvious outsider, a tall man, soberly dressed, with a thin, sad face.

Turning back, Jason asked, "Did you really invite him or did he invite himself?"

"I dunno. Clever sods, the cops. That one, he was here for hours yesterday. He *grilled* me, love. Asked a thousand questions. Friends, where Harry was, the whole bit."

"What did you tell him?"

"To shove it—in a friendly way, of course. He's not a bad guy. But I wasn't going to give him lists of names and have my friends bothered. I told him I didn't know a single person really well."

"How did he react?"

"You're awfully serious, Jason. Get stoned. The cop, I think my indifference convinced him I hadn't been hiding Elsie Vanetti somewhere."

Jason forced a laugh. Conveniently, another guest came and broke into the duologue. Jason eased back. He decided to leave at once. Circling to the door, he edged out of the room with his back to the policeman.

In the hall he was grabbed by an acquaintance. "Bloody Jason. Have some champagne."

For the sake of peace, Jason allowed his mug to be filled. He shook his head when the other man asked if he'd seen Harry yet. "Come on, then, son. Must see Harry. Harry's one of the best."

Jason was bustled into the living room. To have protested, broken away, would have caused an unwelcome scene.

Harry Prentice, plump, bald and rosy-cheeked, was surrounded by men, some of whom were singing a rugby song. One man was balancing a champagne bottle on his head.

Jason and the host shouted greetings at each other, made signs, laughed. His captor stumbling away, Jason left with a lying signal to Harry that he was going to get more champagne.

Out in the hall he moved toward the stairs. He said hello to people, was introduced to others, was kissed by a girl he didn't know. His head was beginning to ache with the noise and cigarette smoke.

There were more greetings and introductions on the way downstairs. Some people Jason stopped to talk to. It would have been strange otherwise. Near the bottom, someone said, "Meet Mrs Greenwich."

Jason smiled and shook a sweaty hand. He would have moved on at once had the woman not looked so out of place in the younger, casually dressed crowd. Like the man upstairs, she was an obvious outsider.

"What a lovely party," she said. She nodded her glass. "Here's to the Prentice family."

"Yes. Here's to them."

After sipping, Mrs Greenwich smiled shyly. "I'm the president of the Elsie Vanetti fan club, you know."

She was short, sturdy and fifty years old. Her tailored suit was as outmoded as the fox-tail looping her neck, her cosmetics as overdone as the cherries on her hat. She had large eyes in a setting of anxious innocence.

Jason made suitable remarks about the reward. Mrs Greenwich said, "Oh, but didn't I have a time of it with the police."

"Really?"

"That one upstairs, his name's Bart, and the one who's been in the papers, Wilkinson, they came to see me. Twice. They investigated me. It was terribly embarrassing."

"I suppose they thought you could have had something to do with Miss Vanetti's disappearance."

"Exactly," Mrs Greenwich said, darting her head forward on the word as if she felt it couldn't get out without help. "The implication was, I spirited dear Elsie away and then chivvied my members into contributing to a reward. Or, that dear Elsie and I were in it together. Or, that the kidnappers had asked me to offer the reward."

Jason said, "They don't miss a possibility, do they?" He was speaking to himself as much as to the woman.

"But it's all over now, thank heavens. Dear Elsie is back. Soon, I'm sure, she'll be fighting fit again."

"Let's hope so, ma'am."

"Cheers."

When Jason got away, he went back up the stairs. He found the policeman. Bart was still by the bedroom door. His face wore a faint public smile, but his sad eyes were watchful. He appeared entirely sober.

Jason went to him. "Hello. Inspector Bart, is it?"

"Detective Sergeant. Hello."

"I'm Jason Galt."

They shook hands. Jason asked, "What's the latest on Elsie Vanetti's condition?"

"No change, I'm afraid."

"I heard a rumour that the lost-memory thing was a gag. That it's to lull the gang of kidnappers into a sense of security."

"Nice idea, Mr Galt," the policeman said, his eyes making a thorough but dispassionate inventory of Jason's features and dress. "But there's no gang, no kidnapping."

"Genuine amnesia, then?"

"It looks that way."

"Interesting," Jason said. "I have an idea on that myself."

Politely: "Oh?"

A champagne bottle was thrust between them and spouted into their vessels. Jason drank, he said:

"If the doctors can't cure her, I might contact the husband and offer to help. D'you think he'd be willing to listen?"

"I really don't know," the policeman said. He was looking away. He had lost interest.

Jason talked on. He didn't mention hypnotism. He performed Party Bore. When the policeman began to show signs of restlessness, Jason moved off with a casual, "Well, so long."

In the hall he stopped to drink. He was satisfied. He had made himself known as a connexion of Angela Prentice, which was healthier than waiting for it to be discovered later, and he had paved the way for his approach to Hull Rainer.

Mug empty, Jason looked around for more champagne, followed a bottle carrier and got recharged. He smiled. He felt better than he had in days. His constant companion, depression, was leaving, sent on its way by alcohol and the talk with Bart.

Jason emptied his mug, got it refilled, emptied it again.

He went in the living room to listen to the singing. Within five minutes he had joined in. He sang with hard, frowning intensity.

Half an hour later, his mug lost, Jason moved unsteadily back to the hallway. It was time, he felt, to go home. His depression had left him completely. He was filled with a not unpleasant melancholy. He had that lovely warmth of self-pity.

Near the bedroom doorway he halted. Between heads he could see Detective Sergeant Bart. He was talking with two girls.

Looking at the policeman, Jason was taken by a compulsion. It was so strong that he got a physical reaction. His spine stiffened, his stomach muscles clenched to ache-hard.

He wanted to confess.

He felt he must. He yearned to go to Bart and say, "I did it. I abducted Elsie and killed her memory with hypnosis. It was immoral and criminal and degraded. Look upon me with scorn."

The compulsion grew stronger. Jason told himself that confession would remove all his pains. He would be purified. It didn't matter that he would go to prison, because he didn't have a future anyway, not alone, by himself, lonely, unloved. Confession was the answer.

Firmly and determinedly, Jason pushed past the intervening people. He reached the doorway and leaned on the frame. The policeman was two feet away.

"Excuse me," Jason said.

Detective Sergeant Bart glanced around. He turned smartly away and went on talking to the girls.

Jason felt hurt; then shocked. A yelling voice of reason had broken through. His body, uncomfortably hot one second, was wetly chill the next. His mouth sagged open.

Flinging himself back from the doorframe, he lurched around and began to shove roughly through the crowd.

● ● ● ● ● ●

The following night, at home, Jason sat watching television in the reclaimed living room. His spirits were low. This was not connected with his mad intention at the party, which he had dismissed as drunken stupidity. Nor was he affected adversely by having read in the morning paper an item which said Elsie Vanetti had been moved to a psychiatric clinic—that analysis might bring back her memory was an old worry. The emotional low was simply his recent norm.

The TV programme, a play, droned on. Jason was not interested and had forgotten the plot. He would have switched off and found something to read were it not for a post-news interview with, topically, an eminent psychiatrist.

Jason got up, a slouch movement. He left the room, crossed the bare landing and went into the kitchen. Preparing instant coffee, he avoided looking at the high-piled dishes in the sink, just as he avoided wondering why of late he had become that sloppy in his habits.

He was drinking the coffee when he heard the introductory music to the news. Finishing in two gulps, he went back to the living room.

The newscast proceeded. Elsie Vanetti was not mentioned. This, although expected, made Jason sigh heavily. He thought:

Soon. It had to be soon. Every day the case grew dimmer in the public mind. And nothing faded faster than a name in entertainment. Yesterday's household word was tomorrow's jungle silence.

Don't be so bloody cheerful, he chided himself.

The weather man finished, the newscast ended, the scene changed to two men sitting in leather armchairs. The interviewer introduced the psychiatrist, an elderly knight with an emaciated face and a gratingly strong voice. Feed and answer began.

Jason knew it all. He wondered why he had been looking forward to the programme.

Fugue, or amnesia, or loss of memory, was a morbid psychological condition with varying degrees of intensity, the pedantic doctor said in twenty times as many words. It was an hysterical state. The most common cause was shock. A counter-shock, electrical, often procured release. Another cause was repression. Which was to say, the patient's subconscious defence-mechanism had blotted out the unwanted. A soldier might forget his act of cowardice which had taken a friend's life; a mother might forget the severe beating she gave her child; a businessman might forget the fire that made him bankrupt. In respect of time, amnesia could work merely on the event itself, or on every connecting aspect: the soldier represses all his military career, the mother ten years of marriage, the businessman his whole life.

Jason switched off the set and wandered out to the landing. He leaned on the bannisters, arms folded. Roving, his eyes went to the open kitchen doorway and then down to the brick that was now being used for a doorstop.

He thought about self-induced amnesia. As his success with Elsie had been so total, so complete to an almost remarkable degree, Jason wondered if it could have been aided by repression; if, in fine, Elsie's subconscious had been eager to co-operate. Agreed, Elsie was highly susceptible, himself talented and their rapport strong, but the success was still quite extraordinary. The aiding factor could well be the play, Elsie's *something evil*.

Not that it mattered to the scheme, Jason thought. It was scientific rather than personal. He simply did not know enough about hypnosis. Nor did anyone else.

Jason's mind here produced the idea which had come to him once before, that of using his future fame in the cause of hypnotism research. It had made him uncomfortable then; it made him more so now.

He pushed himself off the bannister rail, deciding to go out. He felt confined in the flat. Going briskly downstairs, he questioned if the confinement were not actually within himself, due to his stunted and selfish ambition.

Outdoors he began to walk quickly. He let the idea play. He saw money coming not from theatrical performances but in the shape of grants—from governments, schools, foundations, public subscriptions. He saw it being used to create and operate a laboratory, to employ the finest minds in the field.

Jason no longer felt uncomfortable. He was growing excited. His walk turned to a fast stride. His eyes shone.

The laboratory would be dedicated to one end: empirical evidence in every facet of hypnotism. The answers to many riddles would be found. What was the trance state? Whom did the subject believe the controlling voice to be? Was it possible to destroy will?

The potentials of hypnosis were enormous. It may be that a recidivist's criminal tendencies could be eradicated. It may be possible to cure all diseases of the mind, from neurosis to psychosis.

It may, Jason thought on, be possible to cure via mass hypnosis the diseases of bigotry, intolerance, xenophobia, and racial hatred. Which meant cure a large portion of the world's ills. Mankind would be the beneficiary, not Jason Galt.

He stopped walking. He was unaware of his surroundings. Over him moved a wash of relief. It left him limp.

He had, he realised, decided. The celebrity gained from a successful completion of the scheme, he would use not for his own ends but for science.

Jason took a deep breath. He was surprised and pleased. Though sudden, his decision was absolute. He thought he must have been working toward it for some time, otherwise the final step would not have been so facile.

Jason was no longer depressed. He felt as if he had just been given the solution to a problem. It was as though he were ameliorating a pain by discovering an attention-consuming drive. He had peace, satisfaction.

At a stroll, hands clasped behind, Jason continued his walk. He smiled quietly and worked on details of his new future.

● ● ● ● ● ●

The days passed. In newspapers Elsie Vanetti was mentioned briefly, if at all. Jason still had all the worries regarding the final phase of his scheme, but now they were more of an academic nature than nagging doubts. He ate well, slept better. While not happy, he had found a medium level of contentment.

Often he would smile, in a cafe or walking, when seeing something which reminded him of an anecdote from Elsie's past, a past which had come to seem as real as his own, and sometimes more real. The smile would be wistful.

Ten days after leaving Elsie in Covent Garden, Jason read in the morning paper that her condition was unchanged. The time appeared ripe for Jason to make a move.

At eleven o'clock, he went to a telephone kiosk on a quiet street. He was less nervous than expected, but still tense. He dialled with all the care demanded by the occasion.

The call signal rang. It ended, and a voice said, "Hello. Hull Rainer speaking."

"Good morning, Mr Rainer. My name is Jason Galt. I hope you won't think this odd or presumptuous. The point is, I may be able to help your wife."

"Oh, yes?"

"The idea occurred to me the other night at a party. A celebration given by Mrs Angela Prentice. I know her husband and he invited me. It was after talking there with Mrs Prentice and a Detective Sergeant Bart, that the idea came to me."

"What is this idea, Mr . . . ?"

"Galt. Jason Galt. I thought you might remember the name, Mr Rainer. I was in show business myself a few years ago."

"It doesn't strike a bell, I'm afraid. You were an actor?"

"Hypnotist. I had a stage act. After that, I went into hypnotherapy."

"I see," Hull Rainer said. He drew the last word out, its timbre hinting at interest.

Jason said, "Hypnotherapy, I'm sure I don't need to tell you, is the use of hypnotism in psychoanalysis."

"Yes."

"My idea, Mr Rainer, if other treatment fails, is to try hypnosis on your wife to bring back her memory. In fact, I'm convinced I can do it. I've had some first-class successes with similar problems."

"I see, Mr Galt. Yes, I see."

"There's no progress with your wife, I understand."

"None at all."

Tense, Jason asked bluntly, "Then, how do you feel about letting me try hypnosis?"

"Well . . ."

"I should stress one thing," Jason hurried on. "I have an individual approach, one peculiar to myself. In other words, if hypnosis were to be tried by someone else—and it may have been already at the clinic—there could be failure, where I myself might well succeed."

"I think it sounds very promising," Hull Rainer said, his tone brisk. "How about if I get back to you on this?"

"I'm afraid I can't give you a telephone number at the moment. I'm moving about, freelancing with private cases. But I could call you whenever you like."

"Great. Good deal. Ring me in a couple of days, mm?"

"All right, Mr Rainer, I'll do that. Good-bye for now."

"Good-bye, Mr Galt."

Jason lowered the receiver carefully. His feelings were mixed. He had not been given the urgent summons to come at once, which is what he had vaguely hoped for; on the other hand, he had not been dismissed summarily as a crank.

The call had worked as well as reason could expect, Jason told himself. He would have to wait.

Empty but not sad, he headed back to his lonely flat.

16

The clinic was a Regency house which once upon a time had stood in rolling countryside. Although the land was reduced to one acre, there remained an appearance of the manor, a rim of tall elms hiding the upstart neighbours.

Hull Rainer drove slowly along the gravel driveway. He was in no hurry. These evening visits to Elsie had become a chore. It wasn't easy forcing conversation with a mental stranger. Hull resented the obligation. Not only was it a bore, it interfered with his plans. Right now he should be studying the first two scripts of the television series, memorising lines while getting ready for his date with the girl he had picked up yesterday in a Chelsea pub.

Hull looked at his watch. He would make the visit shorter than usual tonight, he decided. Marlene, the doll, was worth a bit of extra effort. She would fill the gap nicely until Simone returned.

Nan Mountford came into Hull's thoughts as he swung around the gravel forecourt. He dismissed her quickly. It made him nervous to recall the scene of a few nights ago, when, after lovemaking, he had suddenly started calling her a whore.

Parking with other cars, Hull went into the lobby. Well and unclinicly furnished in period, it looked like a country hotel.

A nurse and a woman looked around from the reception table as Hull entered. The woman came forward at once. She wore an absurd hat.

Surprisingly, she spread her arms wide and exclaimed, beaming, "She's getting better, Mr Rainer!"

Hull placed her now, having met her twice before. She was the president of the Elsie Vanetti fan club.

"Hello, Mrs Greenwich."

"How do you *do*, Mr Rainer," she said, taking his hand in both of hers. "I'm so happy. It's gorgeous. It's the most wonderful thing that ever happened to me."

"*What* is?"

"Dear Elsie. She's getting better!"

"Really?"

A vigorous nod: "And I'm the first. I started it. I went in there just now and she shouted, 'I know you! You're Mrs Greenwich!' And then she burst into tears. The poor darling."

Hull withdrew his hand. "Her memory's come back?"

"Well, not exactly. Not quite. But it's a start, you see."

"Sure."

"The doctor came and we all talked and it seemed that dear Elsie couldn't remember much else about me. She didn't know anything about the club, her thousands of fans. But she did recall having lunch with me on several occasions."

"Odd."

"Well, it's a start. She's on the mend. And just think, it all began with me."

The nurse, who had been standing nearby, said, "Dr Smith would like to see you, Mr Rainer. He's in his office."

"Fine. Thanks."

Hull had to listen to more of Mrs Greenwich's beaming optimism before getting free and going to the office of Dr Smith. The psychiatrist was a tall, gangly man with awkward movements. His suit was too small. He had a hook-nosed face and quick eyes.

After the men shook hands, Dr Smith put Hull in a chair and himself perched on the desk. He asked, "You saw Mrs Greenwich? She told you about your wife?"

"Yes. It sounds good."

Dr Smith shrugged. "Time will tell, Mr Rainer. What this has done is sway me toward an idea I've been playing with. One regarding Miss Vanetti."

"Her treatment?"

"Sort of. As you know, we've made no progress so far. We've tried mild electric shock, free association and gentle, patient questioning. We've tried a sodium pentathol variant, one of the so-called 'truth' drugs. We're only just getting warmed up, you might say, but actually I'm worried."

Hull folded his arms. "What's the problem, Doctor?"

"I'm concerned that we may be creating in your wife an anxiety state—in addition to the one she has already. That one is quite natural—who wouldn't be worried in her place? But the other she can do without. It might prosper if we push her too hard. She needs a break."

"I see."

"And the break," the psychiatrist said, "might very well do our job for us."

"Cure her?"

"Yes, Mr Rainer. I'd like you to take her home. I want her to be among familiar surroundings and I want her to see as many people as possible—without making it a parade. There could be more recognitions, as with Mrs Greenwich. One might help another, and gradually build up the whole picture."

Without enthusiasm, Hull said, "That could work, I guess."

"I'd like to try it for three or four weeks. If results are negative, we'll get back to work. All right?"

Hull nodded. Next, realising he should be showing pleasure at the change, he said, smiling, "It'll be great to have her home again."

"Of course. And, you know, even if she does get her memory back, in part or whole, she'll still need treatment, analysis, to find out why she lost it in the first place. Otherwise, it could happen again."

"Yes."

"But don't worry, that's outpatient stuff. You'd still have her at home."

"Ah."

"Now, Mr Rainer, I have some papers here for you to sign."

One hour later, Hull was ushering his wife into the Lancaster Gate flat. She wore the blue trouser suit he had fetched from home for her trip from hospital to clinic, and which she had worn there for afternoon walks. Elsie's hair was sleek. She looked and acted like a girl arriving for a job interview.

Hands nervously intertwined at her waist, she gazed around the living room.

"Explore, darling," Hull said. "Do whatever you like. This is your home."

Elsie moved slowly around the room. She touched objects, examined pictures, looked out of the window.

Hull was thinking sourly that right now his date, Marlene, would be pacing annoyedly at the rendezvous, and there was no way to make contact in order to call off the drink-dinner-bed plan. So that was that. He was out with Marlene before he'd been in.

Still sour-minded, Hull thought of the inconvenience of Elsie's continuing presence. It could be months before she got better and started going out on her own, started work again. Furthermore, a slow return of her memory was not worth a damn as publicity. It was not dramatic enough. It . . .

An exclamation broke into Hull's thoughts. He looked about. Elsie was no longer here. He went along to the bedroom.

There, Elsie was looking at his crimson robe lying on a chair. She turned to him with glad eyes.

"I know that," she said. "I bought it, didn't I?"

"Yes you did. In Bond Street."

"I remember picking it off a rack and paying for it with a check." She shook her head. "But nothing else."

"Don't force it."

Elsie strolled away. "This is your room?"

"And yours. We sleep here together."

She turned slowly from looking at the double bed. "Oh," she said dully.

He smiled. "Does the thought bother you?"

Lowering her eyes to the clasped hands, which were nervous again, Elsie said, "I don't know. I—"

"Forget it. There's a guest room I can use. We've got plenty of time."

She looked up, came to him, touched his arm. "I'm sorry. This must be awful for you. I keep thinking of poor me, but for you it must be worse."

He shrugged. Elsie asked, using his name with hesitation, as always, "Hull, do you love me?"

"Well, yes, darling, of course."

"I'm sorry. Please be patient."

"Sure," he said. "Let's have a drink."

"All right. What do I drink?"

"Sherry."

Later, they had a snack. Later still they retired. Hull went drearily into the guest room. Everything had gone flat. He was even being denied sex with his own wife, which, since he was a stranger to her, might have been interesting.

Hull slept fitfully.

The next morning, he was studying his TV scripts and glancing with irritation at Elsie, who wandered about like a wraith, when the telephone rang.

Hull lifted the receiver. His face cleared. He said, "Glad you called, Mr Galt. Yes, I'm interested. I'd like to hear more about this thing. Could you call here later today? Three o'clock?"

● ● ● ● ● ●

"Franz Anton Mesmer was the first big name in hypnosis," the man said, "if we discount Paracelsus. He had a great deal of showmanship, which ultimately clouded over his achievements, and it's possible he didn't fully realise himself what he was doing."

Hull said, "Fascinating."

"As early as 1841, a Dr Ward claimed to have amputated the leg of a hypnotised subject."

"Really?"

They were in the living room, facing each other on couches. Hull was pleased he had asked Elsie not to be present. As she had expressed doubt at what she called mumbo-jumbo, after he had explained what he knew of hypnotism, she would not have been a sympathetic listener.

Hull was also pleased with the manner and appearance of this Jason Galt—good ring to that name as well. Young and good-looking, decently dressed, he had magnetism without being too theatrical, phony-looking. He would, in fact, do very nicely.

Galt said, "But the first consciously induced trance, using methods still used today, was brought about by an Englishman named James Braid. That was over one hundred years ago."

"So this is hardly a new field."

"Not at all," Galt said. He went on talking in an assured manner. He mentioned names which meant nothing to Hull—Liebeault, Charcot, Bernheim—and gave an exegesis of hypnotism's history. It was some time before Hull was able to ask:

"In what way can this be useful to my wife, Mr Galt?"

The hypnotist leaned forward and clasped his hands. "What I would do is put Miss Vanetti into a deep trance. I would open her subconscious. Her memory isn't lost, it's merely hidden, blocked. I would bring it all back to her."

"That would take some time, I imagine."

"One day should be enough."

"Is that all?"

Galt nodded. "Releasing certain key people and places should bring everything else into focus."

"What then? You snap your fingers and she comes awake and remembers everything?"

"More or less. But for safety, to prevent trauma, I'd want certain conditions."

"Go on," Hull said, intrigued.

"I'd want to bring her out of the trance by the stage door of the theatre, at about eleven at night, when everyone's gone. That's the time and place where, assumedly, her memory went. She'll be back exactly where she left off."

"Yes, I follow."

"I'd like her in the same clothes as then. Would that be possible?"

Hull said, "Sure. I've had all her stuff cleaned." He thought how wonderfully newsworthy all this sounded. "Only the scarf's missing. But I can get another the same or similar."

"That's fine."

"What then?"

"Nothing really. If I'm successful, and I feel confident of that, Miss Vanetti will know nothing of what has intervened. She can be told about it slowly."

"Sounds good."

"Could you be there as well, at the stage door, as if meeting her normally?"

"Of course. I was supposed to meet her that night anyway."

"Perfect."

"But you'll be there too," Hull said. "Do I say you're a friend?"

Galt shook his head. "I'll hide nearby before bringing her out of her trance. Everything should be as normal as possible."

"Yes," Hull said. "Yes." He got up and strolled over to the window. After looking out for a moment, he turned and asked, wearing a friendly grin to lighten his words:

"As the saying goes, Mr Galt, what's in it for you?"

"There'd be my fee. Perhaps fifty guineas, if that's not too high."

"No. Fair enough."

Galt smiled. "And there'd be the public fact of my success, which would be a professional advantage."

Hull liked that. He and Galt might almost have been working to the same end. It was beautiful.

Hull said, "Publicity never hurt anyone."

"Good publicity, no."

"You won't mind, then, if I arrange for reporters to be there. I have a contractual agreement, you see, with the *Sunday Standard*."

"As long as they're not close. Not right at the stage door. Is it on the street, by the way?"

"In a yard. Convenient for us. The reporters could wait along the alley."

"Yes."

Hull came back to stand by the couch. "Also, I've promised to let the police know of any new development. Would you object to Wilkinson and Bart being present?"

"Not at all. As long as we can explain all these people to Elsie—Miss Vanetti."

"No need. She'll think they're all pressmen. Nothing unusual in that."

"All right, Mr Rainer," the hypnotist said. "That leaves one final question, assuming you want me to go ahead with this. When do we do it?"

"Anytime you like."

"Tomorrow?"

"I don't see why not. Come along and meet my wife."

17

Jason was tense. The grip came on him as he got up to follow Hull Rainer out of the living room. Up to that point, Jason had been relaxed, far more so than he had imagined he would be.

For one thing, Rainer had not been skeptical. For another, he had gone along with every suggestion—the unnecessary but dramatic choice of time and place and clothing—and had even himself wanted media people nearby. It had all gone unbelievably well.

"This way," Rainer said.

They went into another room. The first thing Jason saw was a double bed. He wondered if . . . But that was nothing to do with him.

He saw Elsie. She was in a corner, at an ensemble of coffee table and two easy chairs. She rose, smiling politely. Her hair was golden and beautiful, her dark-blue dress fitted closely, her face had just enough make-up to highlight her beauty.

Jason felt strange. He couldn't stop looking at her and was both alarmed and exhilarated that she was looking at him with the same concentration. Only vaguely did he hear Rainer's introduction, him saying he would let them talk, his leaving. Jason felt so strange that he wondered if the strain of the past days was beginning to tell.

Next he knew, he was sitting opposite Elsie and answering her question with:

"No, Miss Vanetti, we haven't met before." He spoke in a low voice.

"Curious," she said, speaking as softly, and still searching his face. "I have the strong feeling that I know you."

"That's interesting."

"Yet you aren't really familiar. With Mrs Greenwich it was recognition. With you, it's just a feeling."

"Yes?"

"And your voice. There's something about it."

"Perhaps I remind you of someone you once knew."

She smiled plaintively. "Perhaps."

"Miss Vanetti," Jason said. "I believe I can help you regain your memory."

"Hull told me. With hypnotism."

"Yes. What do you think of the idea?"

"Well, I was doubtful before. I'm not now."

Jason said, "Let me explain what your husband and I have discussed." He did so, briefly, and ended. "Do you think you could trust me?"

She nodded slowly. "Yes. Yes, I do."

"I'd like to spend all day here with you tomorrow. I hope that's agreeable to you."

"Yes."

"Thank you. Thank you very much."

She looked surprised at his thanks. He felt surprised himself.

Elsie smiled. "I should be saying that."

"It would make me very happy to help you."

She leaned closer, again with that searching look. "You must tell me more about yourself. Who you are. Where you're from."

Jason was tempted. He wanted to go on sitting here, talking, listening. But he sensed danger. He didn't know where exactly. It was as if it came from himself, as though he feared he might suddenly start telling the truth about his scheme.

He rose. "Tomorrow, Miss Vanetti. Now I have to go. Will you be ready at nine in the morning?"

"Yes." She got up and gave him her hand. "Good-bye for now, Mr Galt."

"Good-bye for now."

Then, after conferring briefly with Rainer, Jason was out in the street. He was dazed at the swiftness of it all. Dazed and elated. He told himself he had triumphed—and he marvelled at how wonderful this made him feel.

An upthrust in his stride, Jason walked all the way home to Camden Town.

He spent a happily restless evening. The flat was no longer the place of gloom it had been over the past days. He swept the floors, tidied around, washed dishes.

Whistling, he prepared an elaborate meal from all the odds and ends in the ancient refrigerator. In a cupboard he found, stragglers of some forgotten party, a half bottle of red wine and a quarter bottle of white. These he blended to a rosé, which he set to chilling.

He ate like the King of the Poor, alone in his shabby living room, cutlery bent and plates whose cracks had the brown edging of age, wine bottle in a disused chamber pot filled with ice. He ate royally.

Jason felt sure he would be too stimulated to sleep. It was like the night before Christmas. The wine, however, served him as a tranquiliser, and when he at last got into bed, he went to sleep before he could begin to worry about not sleeping.

He awoke early. After a bath and coffee, he dressed with even greater care than yesterday in his best suit and tie and new shirt. He left the house.

The new-day air was fresh after a shower of rain. The keenness tingled on Jason's exposed skin as he walked to the Underground. Everything looked different. He gazed about him happily. He had the strong feeling that today was special. It formed a milestone in his life. A new stretch of highway had begun. From here on, all would be bigger and better and finer. It was a new start.

●●●●●●

"Can you hear the bells ringing?"
"Yes."
"Count them, please."
"One, two, three, four, five, six—"
"Fine. Thank you. They've stopped now."

Jason was more than satisfied. Elsie was in a deep trance. Although Jason had not checked his watch before and after, he knew that the journey from awareness to the profound state had been made in record time. Hardly had he begun on repetition before the subject's eyelids had started to droop. The established rapport was working strong.

Jason and Elsie were in the bedroom, its door closed against interruption. Elsie sat upright on the edge of an easy chair. Her hands, lax, lay palm upward on her lap. Her face wore an expression of mild interest, her open eyes were normal.

Jason, who was standing, leaned down and took one of her hands. He raised it to his lips. The kiss seemed appropriate. It was a token of his thanks.

He sat in the other chair and looked at his notes lying on the coffee table. They were all in sequence, ready. Unlike the destruction of recall, resurrection was going to be fairly simple. The apartment, for example, would not have to be mentally toured in detail; a command to remember would suffice. But there was still a great deal of ground to be covered.

Leaning back, Jason said, "Elsie, we are going to discuss your past. We have talked about it before. Then, I told you to forget it. Now I will order you to remember. Is that understood?"

"Yes," she said, looking at him.

"However, you will not remember fully until you are awake. You are in a trance now. You will come awake and remember when I give you the signal. This is that signal. Listen."

Jason whistled a short call. It was like the low, sad cry of a loon. He said, "I'll do it again." After repeating the call, he said, "You will remember that, Elsie, and when you hear it later today you will remember everything else. You will recall every detail of your life right up to the moment, and that moment is being on the steps of the stage entrance to the theatre, leaving after having said good night to the doorman. Let there be no doubt in your mind. You will remember. Correct?"

"Yes."

Jason sighed. He leaned forward over folded arms and said, "Your name is Elsie Vanetti. You were born in Bristol on the twenty-seventh of April in the bedroom of your parents' house . . ."

So it went. Jason talked, talked, talked. Apart from her role as the listener, the absorber, Elsie's only contribution was an affirmative when asked the endlessly repeated, "Have you got that clear?"

Jason supplied names, showed photographs, recounted incidents. As he tired and his voice grew faint, he had to remind himself constantly that he must not skip, that though much of this could be unnecessary—the order to recall everything being enough—it was not worth the risk of failure at the moment of truth and press-noted drama.

He talked on.

Around noon there was a tap on the door. Jason, calling, "One second, please," stuffed all his notes into his pocket. He had decided that saying he had made them last night would not be a reasonable story.

"Come in."

Hull Rainer looked into the room. "About lunch," he said. "I've made sandwiches and tea."

"Fine."

Rainer stared at his wife with curiosity. He whispered, "Is she in a trance?"

"Yes," Jason said shortly, annoyed without knowing why.

"Looks pretty normal to me."

Jason got up and glanced at his watch. "Let's get this meal over with."

A few minutes later, Elsie eating in her room, the two men were lunching at the kitchen table. The host asked about progress.

"Excellent," Jason said. "Miss Vanetti makes a first-class subject."

"I hope you'll have her ready in time."

"I shall."

"Everything's arranged," Rainer said. "The *Sunday Standard*'s sending two reporters and a cameraman. They'll meet us by the alley at eleven."

"I hope they don't talk about this. We don't want a crowd."

Rainer grinned. "Pressmen talk about a coming scoop?"

"I see what you mean."

"Chief Inspector Wilkinson and his side-kick are going to be there as well. Wilkinson didn't sound impressed."

Jason shrugged, eating. It occurred to him that Rainer appeared more like a man arranging a party than planning and hoping for his wife's recovery. But nerves could do that.

"I also called the theatre," Rainer said. "I asked that no one hang around after the show, and that the stage-door light be left on."

"Good point that, the light."

"I said I'd explain later."

"You've been busy, Mr Rainer."

The host waved his sandwich airily. "Which leaves the scarf. I'll get that this afternoon."

"Good."

They ate a while in silence. Although indifferent to the food, having little appetite, Jason was appreciative of the tea. It soothed his parched throat.

Hull Rainer pushed his plate aside. He put his elbows on the table, prayer-formed his hands and said, eyes stern:

"After all this build-up, police and press and whatnot, I do hope we're going to be successful."

Jason felt a stab of dislike for the man. He drained his cup and got up. "That's *my* problem," he said.

He went back to the bedroom, back to talking.

By six o'clock, Jason was finished. There was no more he could do. He was satisfied. His tiredness was relieved by the usual feeling of peace when working with Elsie—which made him comment to himself that there was nothing so gratifying as controlling a good subject.

In the adjoining bathroom he tore up and flushed away his notes. After splashing water on his face, he went to find the host and food. He was hungry now.

More tea and sandwiches were made, Elsie served, the men ate standing in the kitchen. It seemed necessary to stand. Jason realised the other man was feeling as much growing tension as he was himself.

"Two or three hours' more work," Jason lied. "And we'll be ready."

"Good man."

"The scarf?"

"Had trouble with that," Rainer said, chewing. "Went to a dozen shops. Well, five or six. They said there'd been a run on green headscarves lately. The Vanetti bit. Finally got one in Harrod's."

After the meal, Jason returned to Elsie, put her into a medium trance and told her to lie on the bed, sleep. He stretched out on the floor and dozed. Frequently he awoke with a start, checked his watch, dozed again.

At ten he got up, roused Elsie and deepened her trance. At ten-fifteen he fetched Rainer and asked for the clothes.

On the bed were put the coat, dress and shoes which Jason knew so well. Rainer added the scarf from his pocket, a pair of sunglasses from a highboy. He asked if Elsie could manage herself.

"Of course," Jason said, and to Elsie, "Take off your dress and put these things on. Join us in the other room when you're ready."

Rainer said, going to the highboy again, "Forgot the purse."

"It was in her pocket," Jason said. He added quickly, "Or so the doorkeeper reported. I think I read it somewhere."

Rainer returned with the purse. He put it in a pocket of the raincoat. "There."

He and Jason went to the living room. They paced, sat, paced. Rainer asked, "Drink?" Jason declined. They paced without the spates of sitting.

Both men stopped as Elsie appeared in the doorway. She was exactly as she had been the night of her disappearance: coat, headscarf, sunglasses. Jason felt the strangeness.

Rainer asked, "Shall we go?"

Jason said, "Yes."

18

The MGB, its top up, moved at a steady speed along Sussex Gardens. Hull was driving automatically. While tense, he had no excitement. He was beginning to see flaws in this plan of Jason Galt's.

For one thing, the hypnosis might not work, Hull thought, and then he would look a ripe idiot to police and press, who would possibly tend to be shy of future moves. After all, he knew nothing about this Galt character, who could be a total crank like some of the others who had telephoned.

For another thing, did he want Galt's hypnosis to work? Did he want to be back where he was before, playing tenth violin to the famous Elsie, scouting around for roles?

Hull passed the question over. He thought on:

And if Galt did cure the amnesia, the whole deal was wrong. It would be big in the news, but it would have been four times bigger had there been a build-up to tonight, several days of all the beautiful details. This would be a climax without a start, the last act of a play minus the first two.

Hull jabbed out a blast on his horn at a pedestrian. Elsie, he noted, jumped at the sound. He glanced at her in the light from passing cars. She looked, he thought, like a zombie. And—glancing in the rear-view mirror—Galt looked as if he were on his way to a funeral.

Hull drove on. His tension rose. It was due to the unknown. The mystery was within himself. He didn't know how he wanted the evening to turn out.

They came to the West End. Hull turned into the narrow streets of Soho and zagged along them to the far side. He parked in dimness before shuttered stores.

Getting out, he said to Galt, "The theatre's just around the corner." He circled the car, opened the door and helped Elsie alight. The hypnotist followed.

After locking the car, Hull looked at his wristwatch, turning to catch the light of a streetlamp. He said, "We're in good time."

Galt nodded. He took Elsie's arm and they began to walk. Hull, moving to his wife's other side, thought grumpily that it was his place to take her arm, not Galt's.

They turned the corner. Ahead, three hundred feet away, were the lights of Shaftesbury Avenue, a silver promise at the end of the narrow gloom. Halfway along stood a group of men.

The trio walked on. The two groups became one. There was a jumble of introductions.

The reporters were young, hard-faced men in raincoats and trilbies. They looked more like policemen than the two detectives. The one with an ungainly camera said:

"I'd like to take a shot or two now, if that's okay."

Hull nodded as if with reluctance.

While the flashes were going off and the non-press people, as requested, were grouping and regrouping in various combinations, Chief Inspector Wilkinson said:

"I understand you know Angela Prentice, Mr Galt."

The hypnotist said, "Her husband really. Harry."

"You went to their party?"

"Yes. I talked to Mr Bart there. If he remembers."

The junior detective nodded. "I do now."

"That where I got the idea to try hypnosis."

Wilkinson looked into the bowl of his pipe. "Known the Prentices long, have you?"

Hull, impatient, said, "Look, let's get on with this. We can have a question session afterwards, if everything goes to plan. Have you got enough pictures?"

The cameraman said, "For the present."

"Okay. Now, you know the arrangement. You wait here till we come back. Mr Galt tells me that an interruption could spoil everything, so please remember that. Come on."

Hull led the way along the alley.

Above the stage door the naked bulb was glaring. Hull looked around the untidy yard with distaste. He knew it ad nauseum. Here and in similar places he had waited for his wife, played the faithful dog.

Galt said, "If you'll stand there, please."

Hull stayed in the centre of the yard. The hypnotist went on with

Elsie. He took her partway up the steps to the door, then brought her to a stop and turned her around. Standing beside her and leaning close, he began talking softly.

Hull was unable to hear what was being said. He now had little interest. The night air was chill. He wished he had put on an overcoat. Shoving his hands in his jacket pockets, he struggled against urgency and tension.

At last Galt came down the steps. Elsie stayed. She looked exactly as before, like something in a store window, lifeless.

As Galt came across, Hull asked, "Well?"

"She's ready. All she needs is the signal. You stay here."

Hull turned to watch as the hypnotist went on. He moved to a corner, his figure fading to a dim shape in the darkness beside a stack of scenery. Stopping, he hissed, "All right?"

Hull said, "Yes."

"Can you see me?"

"A bit. And only because I know you're there. It's okay."

"Get ready."

Hull turned away to face his wife. From behind him he heard a low, plaintive whistle. It was eerie. It made him shudder.

Elsie, Hull noticed, seemed to have a similar reaction to the sound. There was a swaying movement about the skirt of her coat. Otherwise she hadn't changed.

Hull went slowly to the foot of the steps. He wasn't sure, but he thought her face directed itself toward him as he moved. He stopped.

In a low voice he said, "Hello, Elsie."

She went on standing there, silent and motionless. Yet he was sure now that she was looking at him, watching from behind the dark glasses.

"Darling," he said.

Elsie's head moved. It dipped forward slightly in a nod. She spoke. She said, "You're here."

Hull shuddered again. He said, "Of course."

"I'd hoped."

"It's our anniversary."

"I know that," Elsie said. Her voice was toneless, as if she were reading aloud without interest.

"Happy anniversary, darling."

"Is it happy?"

"Yes. Sure it is."

"It's appropriate, anyway."

Hull felt awkward, unsure of himself. He was also unsure of Elsie, though it seemed certain she had returned to normal. He didn't know what to say next. He tried:

"Well, how are you?"

"Sick."

"What?"

"Sick of you," she said, and now he sensed that the lack of tone in her voice was due to control.

"Darling."

"You son of a bitch."

Hull twitched with shock. He blinked under a frown, said, "Elsie dear."

She said, "You lowest of bastards."

His body was tense from the toes up. He felt unreal. He whispered, "Darling."

"Bastard."

"You're upset."

"Not any more. I'm calm now."

"You don't understand, dear."

"Yes I do," Elsie said. "Everything." She still spoke in a tight, toneless voice. "I know it all."

"What?"

"I know about my pig husband."

"You've been ill, dear."

"Yes. But not now. My mind's clear."

"It's not, it's not."

"Clear and sharp. Made up."

"Keep calm," Hull said, raising his voice.

"I know what I'm doing."

"Elsie."

She said, "It's all over. It began to be all over when I found out. Found the number."

"Number?"

"In your sock. Isn't that absurd? A telephone number in your sock."

"Oh."

"I called it. I talked to the girl. She told me about you. You're a pig."

Hull shook his head. He was dazed and nauseous, and growing angry. "No, Elsie."

"There were others. I followed you sometimes. I saw you go to their homes for hours. Sometimes you took them to the flat. My home."

"It's a mistake. It's a lie."

"Remember those trips of mine to Bristol? I never went. I followed you, watched you, talked to the girls when you'd finished with them."

Hull couldn't stand these words being said without a matching emotion. It was ugly. She should be shouting. And he remembered the listener in the corner.

He said, "Let's go home."

Elsie came down a step. "It ends here."

"Come on."

"My father would have understood."

"You don't know what you're saying. You're ill."

She shook her head. "No."

"All these lies. I've been faithful to you."

"Lying pig."

"Darling."

"Liar, fornicator, bully," Elsie said in a drone, the tightness of control more pronounced. She came down another step.

"No, Elsie."

"But one's enough. Cheating. You shouldn't have done that. You should have realised who I was."

"You're talking . . ."

"You should never have dishonoured me."

"You're talking so . . ."

"I could have taken anything but that."

"You're talking so strangely."

Elsie came off the last step. Hull felt his anger peaking. He said, "Take off those bloody glasses."

"You sound the true you," Elsie said. She lifted a hand to her sunglasses, at the same time bringing the purse from her pocket. "The true, snarling, reviling bastard."

Hull looked into her eyes. Their stare drained his anger.

He said, "You're ill."

"No."

"Yes. I'll explain to you."

"You can't make excuses. I know it all."

"I don't mean that," he said. "Something else."

"It's all over. It ends here."

"Don't be stupid."

"My father would have understood," Elsie said. She put the sunglasses in her pocket and opened the purse.

"Elsie," Hull said.

He started nervously as her purse fell to the ground. He looked up from it. He started again when he saw that Elsie was holding the letter-opener; holding it by the handle like a dagger.

He stared. Voice low and harsh and wondering, he asked, "What's this?"

"You gave it to me. Poetic justice."

"Elsie," he said, and then again, louder, as her arm went jerking up in a blur of movement. "Elsie!"

19

Something evil, Jason thought. *Something evil.*

The rational part of him was able to think this way even while he watched the sudden action, even while his emotions were aghast and amazed.

Something evil.

This was it. She had not been obsessed with the play. He had been wrong. The obsession was not connected with an existing reality.

With a taste at the back of his throat like blood, Jason watched Hull Rainer jerk backwards and the letter-opener weapon miss his chest by an inch.

She had been planning the kill. She knew it was evil. She both wanted it and feared it. The fear was for self, the want was ethnic—justice of the knife.

Jason stared on in horror as Elsie went forward, intent on Hull Rainer, her weapon again raised above her shoulder.

That was why the something evil had been untouchable, why it had remained in her mind. It was not a memory. It was only a dreaded hope.

Elsie was closing in on her husband, who had been brought to a stop by the scenery at his back. Rainer's face was slack, disbelieving, frightened. His forward-held hands were trembling.

So did it mean that her amnesia had been partially and perhaps wholly self-induced, once suggestion had started? That the hypnotic work had merely been the catalyst, not the overall power?

There was three feet of space between Elsie Vanetti and her husband. The knife was up. Hull Rainer was cringing.

Jason became alert. He snapped from cogitation and from his stupor of surprise. Swiftly he left the corner, calling a sharp, "Elsie!"

She paused, swung her head.

Jason spoke her name again, now in a lower, firmer tone. She stared at him. She was ugly with hate; it was as much for the interruption as for her design.

Jason stopped at her side. The atmosphere was aching with tension, like a scream. Elsie stared, her mouth trying to form words. Hull Rainer gaped and trembled, his face slick with sweat.

Jason knew what he had to do. It was the only way to keep Elsie from going through with her intention—not just now but in the future. Killing Hull Rainer would be her ruin.

And doing what he must would, Jason realised, be his own ruin; as regarded his scheme.

So should he do it? Should he not put himself first?

Jason's indecision was brief. He made up his mind.

"Elsie," he said quietly. "Look at the knife. Look at it now. Knife, Elsie, knife."

Her eyes wavered. She mumbled, "What?"

"Look at the knife. The knife in your hand."

Slowly, face puzzled, Elsie brought the letter-opener around to meet her gaze. Her attention was fixed. Jason said persuasively:

"Look and listen, look and listen. Listen to your father, Elsie. Look at safety and listen to the voice of your father."

The lines on her face began to slacken. She said, "Yes."

"You are safe," Jason said. "You want to be safe. Close your eyes and you will be safe. Close your eyes."

She went on staring at the knife.

"Close . . . your . . . eyes," Jason said slowly, firmly. "It will make you safe. Trust me. Trust your father. Close eyes."

Her eyelids fluttered, lowered.

Jason drew a deep, shaky breath. A similar sound came from Hull Rainer, who sagged back against the scenery and lifted unsteady hands to his face.

Jason set about putting Elsie into a deep trance.

She went there swiftly. Her features relaxed.

Jason said, "You will forget what has happened. When you wake up you will remember only that you came here tonight to try an experiment. That is all. Do you understand?"

"Yes," Elsie said.

Jason took the knife from her hand. He put it in the purse and from there brought the sunglasses. He fitted them to Elsie's face, saying:

"Now, when I snap my fingers, you will come awake. Turn around, please."

Elsie turned. Taking her elbow, Jason led her to the steps, up, and left her there in the same position as before. He retreated, paused for a moment—a moment of regret—and then snapped his fingers.

Movement passed over Elsie's body. She turned her head slowly, then quickly, glancing all around. She looked at Jason. She looked over at Hull Rainer.

She sighed. "Oh," she murmured. "Nothing's changed. I—"

Rainer broke in. Coming forward in a hesitant walk, he said, voice husky, speech without balance, "Listen. I've got to go. I've something to do. Urgent. I'm late. You'll be all right, Elsie. I'm leaving. I'll, I'll . . ." Fumbling off, he strode swiftly across the yard and into the alley.

Elsie looked at Jason. She asked, "What's wrong?"

He shrugged.

"Is Hull angry because the experiment failed?"

"Perhaps," Jason said. "It could be something else." He held out his hand. "Come along."

She came down the steps and over to where he stood. Smiling reassuringly, he took her arm. They began to walk.

Jason said as they went along the alley, "You know, I have a feeling that you won't be seeing much of your husband from now on."

"Oh?"

"I hope you won't be too hurt by that."

Elsie shook her head. "I don't know. I don't even know how I feel about Hull. He's a stranger. Maybe he's the one who's going to be hurt."

"I doubt it."

Then they were out on the street with the policemen and the reporters, and all was a confusion of voices: questions about what had happened and why Rainer had left so abruptly.

"Looked scared stiff," one of the reporters said.

Brushing over that, Jason heard himself admitting that the experiment had failed, that his hypnotic powers had not been strong enough.

There was more talk. There was also muffled laughter; laughter with a ring of derision which made Jason cringe inside. He longed to shout the truth. He dare not.

The group broke up. The reporters strolled off. The detectives, after shaking hands warmly with Elsie and briefly with Jason, went in the other direction.

Still arm in arm, Jason and Elsie walked along toward Shaftesbury Avenue. In the brightness there, Jason waved at a passing cab. He opened the door when the taxi halted at the kerb, and handed Elsie in.

He said, "Don't be too disappointed in my failure. It could be for the best."

"But what happens now?"

"Go home. Rest. Start planning a new life. Get someone to stay with you, if you like. Your mother, a friend."

She leaned forward on the seat. "I don't know my mother. I don't know my friends."

"You'll get to know everyone, starting from scratch."

"And you, will you contact me?"

He nodded. "Yes. I'd like to."

"Soon?"

"Very soon."

They smiled gently at each other. Elsie said, "Perhaps we can try again with hypnosis."

"Perhaps," he said. But he knew he never would.

Elsie said, "Good night, then."

"Good night."

He closed the door, the cab moved away. Elsie turned to wave through the rear window.

When the taxi had gone from sight, Jason walked on. He felt sad, yet at the same time oddly elated. His scheme had failed, but not his gift. And there was Elsie. She was safe now, and she stood a chance of gaining the one thing she had always wanted: to be happy.

Jason's walk became firm. He looked at the lights above. They seemed to signify the loneliness of a success which no one would ever know about except himself and Hull Rainer.

Jason was alone but proud; and hopeful.